Anonymous

Childrens' Holidays

a story-book for the whole year

Anonymous

Childrens' Holidays
a story-book for the whole year

ISBN/EAN: 9783337287467

Printed in Europe, USA, Canada, Australia, Japan

Cover: Foto ©Andreas Hilbeck / pixelio.de

More available books at **www.hansebooks.com**

CHILDRENS' HOLIDAYS:

A

Story-Book for the whole Year.

NEW YORK:

D. APPLETON & COMPANY,

413 & 415 BROADWAY.

1865.

CONTENTS.

HOLIDAYS.

NEW-YEAR'S DAY.

I HAD not seen my friend, Mrs. Howard, since we parted as classmates, twenty years before, having "finished the course" at our boarding-school. I had, however, often heard of her as a happy wife and mother, and from time to time had received from her kind messages and words of sympathy. For my own lot had been a different one. Friend after friend had been taken from me, and I was now almost alone in the world.

On the afternoon of the last day of the year, I was detained by a railroad accident, in the beautiful village where she lived. I was compelled to choose between spending the night at L——, and travelling alone till midnight.

I preferred to remain till the next day, especially as I should thus have the opportunity of seeing my old friend. After tea my landlord provided me with an attendant to her residence. As we walked up the long path to the door, I could see in the moonlight that it was a large house, surrounded by a lawn, which was shaded by fine old elms, oaks and weeping willows. The door-bell was answered by a neat waiting-maid, and I was ushered into a large, handsome room, warmed and cheered by a blazing wood-fire. A lady sat at the centre-table reading. She rose at my entrance, evidently not quite recognizing her visitor : "Mary Williams !" said I at last.

I Received a Cordial Welcome.

"Why, Anna Sanford, you dear girl!" she exclaimed, embracing me.

A most cordial welcome I received, and so urgent an invitation to spend the night, and to stay over New-Year's, that I had no heart to decline it.

"My babies are all asleep," said Mary, " they have gone to bed early, so as to be sure and wake up as early as possible. But you will see and hear enough of them in the morning."

We had a long talk that evening of the old school-days, and the later joys and sorrows. Mary, too, had been afflicted. Her eldest daughter had been taken from her by a very sudden and distressing death, and another child had died in infancy. I thought I could trace the effect of these sorrows in a tender, thoughtful manner, which added new grace to her former loveliness.

At last we parted near midnight, and I went

to my pleasant room, warmed like the parlor by a blazing wood-fire. I sat and thought of life and its changes, and of God's care over us all, appointing unto each his different lot, in the same infinite love. And I gave myself anew to be His; to live not in my own joys and sorrows, but for Him and his kingdom.

I was wakened long before light by some one opening the door of my room, and a merry voice wishing me "a Happy New-Year." By the lamp in the passage, I could dimly discern a little curly-headed, white-robed creature, pulling down the coverings, and preparing to jump into my bed. Not quite recollecting where I was, I asked, "Who is that? What do you want?" I suppose the strange voice frightened the child, who instantly replied—suiting the action to the word,—"Oh, ma'am, I want to cover you up," and then scampered from the room.

I heard her say in the passage, "It isn't Aunt Anna Gray, it's somebody I don't know."

I laughed heartily, and being by this time thoroughly wakened, I opened the door, and gave my New-Year's greeting to the two little girls, whom I discovered standing in their night-gowns, discussing the question who the stranger could be. Though somewhat shy at first, they were at last induced, partly by my entreaties, and as much probably by the cold, to make me a visit in my warm bed. There we had a long chat: about mamma, and papa, who was away; about their brothers and sisters, Bessie, the eldest, and Willy, and Gertrude, and Harold, of whom the two youngest were at this very time paying a similar visit to their mother in *her* bed. They told me about their sister and little brother, who were in heaven; and about Susan, the good old nurse, and Bridget, and Sally, and John; and about the two horses, Romeo and Rolla, who ran away with mamma and Uncle Henry a few days before; and about the cow, and the new calf, "pure white, a perfect beauty;" and about Willy's dog Carlo, and Mary's maltese kitty, Cora; and Bessie's canary, Cherry; and Maggie's beautiful white rabbit, Bunny; and about their grandfather, who lived near them, and their uncle and aunt who lived with him; and about their flowers in summer, and their sleds in winter; and their school, and their books, and their playthings; and about the Christmas-tree at grandpapa's; and what a "splendid time" they had; and what a "beautiful time" they were going to have to-day, at New-Year's; grandpapa was coming to dinner. "I don't think we shall have any presents," said Maggy, "because we had so many at Christmas." "Did you ever see my grandfather?" asked Mary, suddenly.

I replied that I had never seen him, but had often heard what a good man he was.

"Well," said Mary emphatically, "he is the handsomest man I ever saw; I don't see any body else so handsome any where. He looks so kind and good, and his curls look like silver, hanging down his shoulders."

And so the little prattlers entertained me till after daylight, when I enjoyed a new pleasure in looking at their bright, happy faces.

Before the first bell rang, they had gone to dress themselves, and "run over to grandpapa's, to wish them all a Happy New-Year before breakfast."

The morning dawned calm and bright, as if the solemn midnight had not closed over the joys and sorrows, and irrevocable deeds of another year; as if the mysterious angel of the new year had not, in that dark silence, commenced his course, bearing in his right hand changes of deep import for us all.

I threw open the window, and looked out upon the new day. There had been a fall of snow in the night, and far and wide over the broad landscape lay its soft, white mantle. The dark branches of the cedars hung drooping under its weight; the bushes were shaking off their unwonted burden, fences were tipped, and houses were roofed with pure white marble. All steps of men, and all defilements were covered up and out of sight. The pure, unspotted snow ushered in the new and untried year.

I found my friend in the cheerful breakfast-room seated in a large chair, with her beautiful little Harold on her knee, and the whole group of merry children in animated talk around her.

I was introduced to them all,—Bessy, the eldest, a girl of twelve, with eyes and hair like her mother's; Willy, a fine little fellow of nine; then my little friends, Mary and Maggy, who assumed the air of old acquaintances, in virtue of their morning visit; then little Gertrude, with her blue eyes and long curls, and lisping prattle which won her the title of " Chatterbox ;" and last, yet not in all respects least, Master Harold, the baby, the darling of the house.

" You are rich, Mary," said I.

" I am indeed," she answered, adding with emotion after a moment's pause, " I have treasures too laid up in heaven."

" Where no moth corrupteth, nor thief approacheth," I ventured to reply.

" Yes, I am thankful that they are safe ; but the recollection of them is very fresh this New Year's morning. Two years ago our little George was with us."

Bessy drew gently near, and stood with one arm round her mother, her face expressing the tenderest love and sympathy.

Mrs. Howard evidently made a strong effort to be composed.

"Bessy, dear," said she, "after breakfast you must show Miss Sanford the daguerreotype of little George. Now we must not let the thought of him make us unhappy."

"I know it, mother, but it is so hard to think of him in the cold ground, so happy! so beautiful!"

"But he is not in the cold ground, my love, he is where all is beautiful, and happy and holy."

"It makes every thing seem so uncertain to me," said Bessy.

"It should not, my love. Nothing can come except what our Heavenly Father permits; we cannot escape from His care any more than we can escape from His power. We must not shrink from what He sends, nor should we suffer the thought of what may come to us to disturb our present peace."

"How can we be happy when we think of sorrow and death?" asked Bessy.

"Sorrow and death are real," replied her mother, "and there is no true happiness in shutting our eyes to realities. But there are other realities which we should also remember,—God, and His care and wisdom, and the life to come. It is a great thing," she added, turning to me, "to have our habitual views of life include sorrow as well as joy, so that it shall be no stranger when it comes to us."

"And so that we may then remember that there is joy as well as sorrow," replied I. "The danger with us all is of making the present experience too engrossing. We are not far-sighted enough, we see only the dark or bright thread passing though our fingers, without considering how it is to be woven into the web of life ; it is the dark shades which give the richness to the finished work."

We were summoned to the breakfast table. As a great privilege of New-Year's morning, little Harold was allowed to be present, and Miss Gertrude was very officious in arranging for him her high chair, and in seating herself on a large book in a lower one. A beautiful group they were, from the mother down to the bright-haired baby at her side.

After breakfast Mary took the Bible, remarking, " I make no stranger of you, Anna. Where is the place, Maggy ?"

Maggy named the fifteenth chapter of John, and the other children read in turn ; then we knelt, and in brief and simple language, the mother offered a prayer of thanksgiving for the past, of trust for the future, of consecration of her household to Christ and His service,—a prayer which revealed, while it was far from displaying, a heart whose habitual life was near to God.

When we rose, the children each came in turn with a kiss to mamma, and I was so happy as to receive a similar favor from all but little Gertrude, who, tossing back her curls with an air of dignity, said, " No, I don't kiss any body but my own folks." She lingered in her mother's arms, and, looking up roguishly, said, " I habn't seen my New Eve's present yet, mamma ! "

" But you were not to expect a New-Year's present, you know, " said her mamma. " But I *wish* I *could* have one," persisted little chatterbox.

Her mother smilingly rang the bell, and gave an order in a whisper to the servant.

In a few minutes she said : " Now suppose we all come to the door and enjoy this fine morning."

The little group flocked to the side-door which opened on a verandah. Such exclamations of surprise and delight met my ears that I too hastened to

2

look out.   John was leading a beautiful black pony equipped with a side-saddle.

"Oh, mamma!" said Bessy. "Is that for us?"

"That is a New Year's present from papa to all his dear children."

"What a beautiful creature!   When did it come?"

"It has been in town several days at a livery-stable.   Your papa sent it with directions that it should be kept there till New-Year's morning."

The delight of the children was unbounded. Each must mount and have a ride, and it was the universal opinion that papa was the best papa in the world, and that the pony was the prettiest, and the easiest, and the dearest little pony that ever was seen.

We left the children under John's care to enjoy their new delight, and I was well pleased in being allowed to assist Mrs. Howard in some preparations for dinner; for, as Maggy had said, there was to be a family party.

Susan, the nurse, soon followed us, eager to tell Gertrude's "last speech." She had been standing at the nursery window, and shook her head at Gertrude to prevent her walking in the snow, as her rubbers were worn out. Gertrude hesitated, longing to go to the pony, yet not daring to disobey. Suddenly she ran into the kitchen to Bridget, and said, "Bridget, you go into the nursery and hold Susy's head, so I can go and see the pony." Bridget took the little chatterbox in her arms, and, in spite of Susy's head, carried her out, and seated her in triumph on the pony's back.

At eleven the sleigh was at the door, and Mrs. Howard and myself, with the younger children, took a drive about the beautiful village. The air was clear

and exhilarating, and the new-fallen snow gave fresh-
ness and purity to the landscape. We were all in
fine spirits, and the horses seemed to have caught
the infection, for they bounded on as if solely for
their own pleasure.

Mrs. Howard pointed out fine old trees, distant
mountains, handsome residences, and public build-
ings, and what interested me most, the Cemetery,
where her little ones had been laid among many of
the loved and honored.

We returned only a few moments before one,
the dinner hour. When I came down to the parlor,
I found Judge Williams and his family already there.
I could quite understand and share Maggy's admiration of her grandfather. His youngest daughter was
a striking likeness of her sister, Mrs. Howard, as I
remembered her twenty years before.

Our sleigh-ride had given us a good appetite for

the enjoyment of the bountiful dinner. The children were all at the table, Gertrude by the side of her grandfather, and little Harold in the high chair next his mother. The father alone was wanting to make the circle and the enjoyment complete.

Willy came in just as we seated ourselves, with a glowing cheek and a bright glance at his mother, which she smilingly returned. I understood its meaning, for, during our slight labors in the kitchen, where the preparations for dinner were exposed, Mrs. Howard had explained to me why two turkeys were to be roasted instead of one. Some months before Willy had had a present of a young turkey, which he had reared with great care, intending it for the New-Year's dinner. He had lately become much interested in a bright little school-mate of his own age, the son of a sick widow. "A few days ago," said Mrs. Howard, " he asked me privately, if it would be right for him to make any other use of the turkey than the one he had designed, and if I thought that James Green's mother would like it if he gave it to them. I gave a very ready assent to his plan as you may suppose, and Bridget is going to have a part in the gift by roasting it."

"And indade, I should have a hard heart to refuse to help a poor widow, let alone the pleasure it will give Master Willy, ma'am," said Bridget.

I discovered, by some pies and jelly set apart for the same destination, that Mrs. Howard also intended to have a share in the pleasure. Willy was to carry them all on his sled, as a present to his friend James, and I knew that he had just returned from his kind errand.

After a long chat over our nuts and raisins, we returned to the parlor, where coffee with the richest of cream was served. After Grandpapa's cup was removed, little Mary stole to his side, and was soon comfortably established upon his knee. I saw him from time to time stroke the shining curls, and once imprint a kiss upon the fair forehead with a sad look, which seemed to me to turn back to years long past, and to another whose beloved name she bore. It was only for a moment, but my heart warmed toward him in reverent sympathy.

" Now tell me a story, *peas*, gampapa," said Gertrude, slipping from her mother's lap, and running towards him.

" No, you must tell *me* one, about the little blackbirds."

Gertrude held up her little fat hands, and spread out her ten fingers and began:

> " Ten little blackbirds sitting on a vine,
> One flew away, and then there were nine.

" Nine little blackbirds sitting on a gate,
One flew away, and then there were eight.

" Eight little blackbirds flying up to heaven,
One flew away, and then there were seven.

" Seven little blackbirds sitting on some sticks,
One flew away, and then there were six.

" Six little blackbirds sitting on a hive,
One flew away, and then there were five.

" Five little blackbirds sitting on a door,
One flew away, and then there were four.

" Four little blackbirds sitting on a tree,
One flew away, and then there were three.

" Three little blackbirds sitting on a shoe,
One flew away, and then there were two.

" Two little blackbirds sitting on a stone,
One flew away, and then there was one.

" One little blackbird sitting all alone,
  He flew away, and then there was none."

" Now gampapa, peas tell me my story."

Her grandpapa kissed the little upturned forehead, and commenced thus :

" Once there was a little boy who was on his
way to school in the morning.   His teacher was very
strict, and punished every scholar who was not at
school in season, that is, at nine o'clock.

" Our little boy started very early with his satchel
on his shoulder, but he had gone only a little way,
when he saw a little dog, who was howling as if in
pain.

" ' What is the matter, little dog ? ' said he.

" ' A carriage has run over my leg,' said the dog.

" ' Never mind, little dog ; jump right into my
satchel.'

" So the dog jumped into his satchel.

" He went a little farther and saw a brook making a great noise, as if complaining as it ran along.

" 'What is the matter, little brook?' said he.

" Some one has been throwing dirt and stones into me,' said the brook.

" ' Never mind, little brook; jump right into my satchel.'

" So the brook jumped into his satchel.

" He went a little farther and saw a horse which was moaning in pain.

" ' What is the matter, poor horse?' said he.

" 'My master has been beating me,' said the horse.

" ' Never mind, poor horse; jump right into my satchel.'

" So the horse jumped into his satchel.

" When the little boy reached the school he was very late,—as much as sixty seconds after nine o'clock. His master looked very sternly at him and said, 'Johnny, come here.'

"Johnny went trembling, with his satchel on his shoulder.

"'Hold out your hand.'

"'Oh! please sir, don't; I started early.'

"'I can't help it, you came *here* late. Hold out your hand.'

"Johnny held out his hand; but before the master could strike a blow, up jumped the little dog and barked terribly at him, 'bow, wow, wow;' and up jumped the brook, and spattered him all over with muddy water; and before he could wipe his eyes to see what was the matter, out jumped the horse and took him on his back, and galloped away with him to the world's end."

Gertrude clapped her hands and said, "it was a boohful story."

"I want a story too," said Mary. "Will you please tell me a story, grandpapa?"

Her grandpapa thought a moment, and said, "I will tell you a riddle, and you may guess it.

> "'Within a wall as white as milk,
> Within a curtain soft as silk,
> Within a river bright and clear—
> A golden apple doth appear.'

"Perhaps Bessy or Willy can tell me what it is."

None of the children could guess it, and if any other children cannot, I presume that their mothers all learned it in their youth, and can tell them the answer to this beautiful riddle.

"I think, Bessy, that we can give grandpapa a riddle too," said Mrs. Howard, "the one that your father sent you."

"Oh, yes!" said Bessy. "Now, grandpapa,"

> " ' Can you tell me why
>   A hypocrite sly
>   Can better descry
>   Than either you or I,
>   Upon how many toes—
>   A pussy-cat goes ? ' "

Her grandfather, her uncle and aunt and I thought for some minutes, until at last all said that we must "give it up," we could not guess it.

> " A sly hypocrite
>   Can best counterfeit (count her feet),
>   And so, I suppose,
>   Can best count her toes."

We laughed heartily, and did not wonder that we had been unable to guess it.

"Now I will give you a charade," said I to Bessy :

" ' Perfect, I am a blow;
        Headless, I am a dish;
        Tailless, I am a fragment,
        As small as you could wish.
        Headless and tailless, I can run;
        Headless again, I rend;
        Transposed, in my perfect state,
        My aid at Church I lend.' "

Miss Williams soon gave the solution—" Stripe, —Tripe—Strip—Trip—Rip—Priest—"

I added that I believed between thirty and forty words could be made from the letters comprised in the word "stripe."

The children were quite incredulous in regard to this assertion, but on taking pencils and paper they were soon convinced; and, in fact, they spelt forty-three words with some or all of the six letters.

" I know some poetry," said Mary, " some that Maggy made."

"What is it?" asked her uncle Henry.

"Oh we must all say it together; come, Bessy, you know; come, children."

There was a good deal of whispering and laughing, and then the children all stood in a row, and said in a singing tone:

> "Grandpa, grandpa, grandpa dear,
> How I love you right down *here*,"

all laying their hands upon their hearts, except little Harold, who placed his a little lower down.

This great performance drew forth universal applause, and was repeated by request of the audience.

And so we sat pleasantly chatting, till the lamps were lighted, and the tea-tray carried round.

After tea, the children claimed of their uncle the fulfilment of his promise to show them "the elephant."

I suppose that I must not tell how it was done; but it was so successful an imitation of the animal in form, color, size and gait, little Harold riding on his back,—that I was as much astonished as any of the children. Gertrude was really frightened by it.

Then we had " the man climbing the wall," an ingenious trick, which, by the arrangement of the shadow from a lamp, represented the ascent of a man above the door, and his descent again.

Then came the game of " hieroglyphics," which puzzled all who did not understand it ; next the game of " scandal," in which a story grew as it passed from mouth to mouth, till it was a very different tale, when it came back to the ears of its originator, from the slight hint with which it had started.

Then we had the game of " statues," in which a rich, but ignorant country gentleman comes to an artist's studio, and the blunders he makes in buying statues for his various niches. Each person representing a statue must sit perfectly motionless, in spite of all the funny things that may be said about him, and if he smiles he is sold immediately.

Then came the " Menagerie."

" Do you know it, Miss Sanford ? " asked Bessy.

I confessed my ignorance.

" That's good," shouted Maggy.

I was ordered into another room, and asked what animal I wished to see.

" A monkey," I decided upon.

I was ushered with ceremony back into the parlor, where Mrs. Howard and her sister stood holding a shawl by the corners as high as they could reach.

" Miss Sanford wished to see a *monkey*," said Bessy, very gravely, " Will you please show her one, mamma ? "

The ladies dropped the shawl, and I saw myself, in a large mirror. 3

We all laughed heartily, and the children thought it an excellent joke.

But nine o'clock came at last, as if it was any other evening, and the children were reminded of bed time. There was no teasing for " a little while longer," but a quick and cheerful obedience, which showed that, while the mother shared the children's pleasures, the children shared the mother's will.

" Perhaps grandpapa will read with us before you go to bed," said Mrs. Howard turning to her father.

" Certainly," he replied.

Mrs. Howard handed him the large Bible, and he read in an impressive manner, the ninetieth Psalm, —"Lord, thou hast been our dwelling place in all generations."

I was touched by his solemnity, and by the reverent manner of the whole group, especially of those young children, turning from the innocent sports which had excited and absorbed them a few moments before, to listen to those words of holy wisdom.

Then we knelt in prayer, and with a depth of feeling which his strong nature usually kept concealed, the venerable man prayed for his children, and his children's children, committing them to the care of a faithful God for the year to come, and for all years, and for eternity. His tenderness showed us how his heart had been turned to the past, and how his hopes were fixed in the world beyond the grave.

And when, after we rose, one grandchild after another went, with loving awe, to receive his kiss and blessing; and Mrs. Howard half playfully, half solemnly said, "I must have one too," I could not restrain my tears, while I felt more deeply than ever before, that I had no father, no mother, no near kindred. Yet my heart could say, "Our Father who art in heaven," and thank him that there were homes like this upon the earth.

MRS. BROWN'S CHILDREN'S PARTY.

"JUST this once, dear mother; you know we never have been to one," pleaded Mary.

Ellen did not speak, but her blue eyes looked volumes of entreaty.

"Why not? What is your objection?" asked my brother from Iowa, who had come for a few days' visit. "I am sure, I should like, myself, to see a children's party, such as we used to have at home. Don't you remember, the famous plays in Mr. Reed's dining-room, and at Squire Dickinson's?—Button, and Hunt the Slipper, and Blind Man's Buff, and

Here we go round the Barberry Bush! I should be very sorry to be without such recollections, or to have my children grow up without them."

"I imagine that children's parties in New York are very different from those," said I, "but I know very little about them. I only know that they are too late in the evening, and I have heard that the refreshments are not at all suitable. Then there is danger of taking cold in coming home, and the excitement will probably upset them for a day or two. These are my chief objections."

"But, mamma," said Mary, "you know Aunt Mary said, that we could go and come back with Willy and Caro, in their carriage; and their nurse will go for them, and see that we are all wrapped up nice and warm."

"How far is it?" asked my brother.

"About half a mile. Now go, little girls, and I will think about it."

" By the way, Edward," said I, after they were gone, " do you remember that pretty girl, Jane Gibbs, who used to stand behind the counter in good old Mrs. Harris's shop ? "

" Mrs. Harris the milliner ? Yes, I remember there was a girl there, and she used to bring home your bonnets. I recollect mother's talking to her one day, and telling her she ought to go to school."

" This Mrs. Brown who is to give the party, is that young girl."

" Is it possible? Well, sister, I think that is another reason why you should accept her invitation. She might feel hurt if you declined."

" I confess I had the same feeling for a moment, but I think if you could see her in her present estate, you would not be long troubled by any such fears."

" I have quite a curiosity to see Jane Gibbs

transformed into a fine lady," replied my brother. " What a country this is ! Liberty and Equality ! If this is a specimen, you have as much of it here as we have at the West. But I do not know any thing against Mrs. Brown, or any reason why our children should not go to her children's party, or why you and I should not go in the course of the evening, and look in upon them."

" I should like to do so, and Mrs. Brown, I dare say, would be pleased to receive a call from you."

So the children received permission to go to the party.

" What shall we wear, mother ? " asked Mary.

" That is easily decided," I replied, " as you have but one nice dress."

" What, our blue thibets ? But cannot we wear low-necked dresses, mamma ? "

" Low-necked dresses, in the middle of January !

What are you thinking about, you crazy little kitten?" said her uncle, playfully shaking her shoulders. "I remember your mother once did that foolish thing, when she was a young lady, and suffered for it for months afterward."

"You need not fear that I have forgotten that folly, brother. No, Mary dear, I cannot think of such a thing as a low-necked or thin dress. You must wear your thibets if you go."

"Cousin Caro is going to wear a low-necked dress," said little Ellen : "she is having one made on purpose, a beauty ; a pink silk with flounces."

"I cannot help what Cousin Caro is to wear ; but my little girls will do as I think best, or else what use is there in having a mamma of their own?"

Mary came and kissed me, and said I was the best mamma in the world, and she would rather please me than wear twenty low-necked dresses ; and

Ellen laughed and said that she would too; and my brother laughed, and gave them each a toss up in the air.

The evening came, and the little ladies were arrayed in their light blue merinos, with lace in the neck and sleeves, and some very pretty muslin aprons, simply embroidered pantalettes, and neatly-fitting gaiters. They looked so fresh and pretty, that I felt, to say the least, no doubt as to their being sufficiently well dressed, and was only afraid that they would be too conscious of it.

I had lived only a short time in New York, and had not many acquaintances in the city. My husband was absent at this time, and my sister-in-law had begged as a favor to her children, that mine might be allowed to accompany them, and said that they should come home in good season.

When her carriage came, it was nearly eight

o'clock, my children's bed-time. We had been long expecting it, as the invitations were for seven. My little girls hurried into it, and off they drove.

"Is it not time for us to go?" asked my brother.

"Not quite, I think, and I must change my dress."

"How absurd for a children's party!"

But I knew Mrs. Brown too well for that, and added to my plain black silk, a dress cap and my best embroideries; and we reached Mrs. Brown's about half-past nine.

The house was lighted from top to toe, and as we rang we heard a band of music within.

"But can this be the place?" asked my brother. "It cannot be."

"O yes, it is; but I am surprised to hear that music."

That, however, was only the small beginning of

surprises. We were formally ushered into the large long drawing-room, and presented to Mrs. Brown. She was one of that class of ladies of whom it would be difficult to say what they would be in themselves; there were so many flowers, and flounces, and ends of ribbons, and bits of finery; so much jewelry and so much manner! She was *delighted* to see Mrs. How-ard, and *extremely* happy to see Mr. Gilman, and extended two white-gloved fingers in a very conde-scending way. I saw one of my brother's queer smiles hovering about his mouth, and was glad to see him turn his head and take a survey of the scene.

But I don't think his face showed any less sur-prise; I did not think of looking to see, so absorbed was I by my own. There were two large parlors full of little ladies and gentlemen in white satin slippers, and white kid gloves, rich silk dresses, trimmed with costly lace, artificial flowers, breast-

pins, bracelets, gold chains and watches, all the dress
and all the airs of grown-up belles and beaux. They
were dancing, all of them, except my own Ellen, and
her favorite little friend, Jeannie Carroll, who were
sitting together, looking wearily and anxiously at the
gay dancers. As soon as Ellen saw me, she sprang
from her seat, and then turned to her companion
and brought her to me.

"But why are you not dancing, too?" asked
my brother.

"Oh, I don't know how," she replied. "I can
only jump, and Jeannie cannot dance, either, so we
were looking on."

"But where is Mary?" asked I, and at the same
moment discovered her, flying towards me, in the
dance. She had not been taught to dance, but her
vivacity and self-assurance, her musical ear and quick
perceptions, supplied the deficiency.

"A beautiful sight, is it not, Mr. Gilman?" asked Mrs. Brown, in a very gracious tone.

"Pardon me, madam, but I think I never saw a sadder one."

"Why, what can you be thinking of?"

That same strange smile was on my brother's face, as he answered solemnly—"I was thinking, madam, of an expression which was once used, '*Of such is the kingdom of heaven.*'"

"Yes, they do look like little angels, I am sure," replied the lady.

I did not dare look at my brother. Fortunately, at that moment, my little niece, Caro, came up to me. I hardly knew the child, at first, in her finery. Somebody had broken her gold chain, and the locket had fallen to the floor and been crushed, and the hair lost. It was the hair of her little brother, who was dead; and the locket contained his miniature. I tried to comfort her, but her peace was gone for the evening.

There were various accidents of the same kind. Three or four handsome bracelets were broken, and one expensive watch was ruined. However, the little gentleman owner declared, with a very careless air, that it was of no sort of consequence ; his father would give him another one the next day.

" Poor children ! " said my brother. " What is there left for them when they grow up, Is this all they know of childhood ?"

Mr. Brown, after rapidly making a large fortune in California, had travelled in Europe for the double purpose of spending and displaying his money. Other gentlemen of fortune bought pictures and statues, and as he was a gentleman of fortune, why should not he ? He valued beauty, as he did other things, by the dollars it cost. Thus, though he possessed some

paintings of great merit and beauty, the gain was
not his, so much as that of some of his guests; for
he was not wise enough to know that beauty is no
private possession, but belongs to all who see and
love it.   But he had paid for them, and they were on
his walls; and very glad was I. My brother walked
round leisurely with me, and made few comments,
but I saw that he was deeply moved, and there was
a sad satire in his smile, as he turned from Madon-
nas, angels, and holy children on the walls, to the
dressed-up, artificial little caricatures on the floor be-
low.   There was one picture—a lovely child, almost
nude, seated on a bank of flowers, looking up and
listening to a bird.   There was a copy of the Bridge-
water Madonna, so pure and unworldly.   There was
a sleeping child, surrounded by angels, who seemed
to be giving it dreams of heaven.   There were the
Babes in the Wood.   There was Christ blessing lit-

tle children, and saying, "Suffer them to come unto me, and forbid them not." There was Christ rebuking his disciples, by setting a little child in the midst of them.   My brother looked intently at this, and then, glancing round over the silks and laces, quietly said, "I wonder if one of these specimens would have answered the purpose." There was Paul preaching at Athens.   There was the Choice of Hercules,—"most a beautiful picture," as Mr. Brown assured me ; and there were many others, all like these, telling of heroic virtue, of free nature, of purity, simplicity or sanctity ; and there, before their very eyes, in contradiction and mockery of their whole intent, was acted this preposterous farce,—this sacrifice of the higher to the lower nature, of the heart of childhood to sense and mammon.

On looking round, I saw my little Ellen and her friend Jeannie standing before the picture I have mentioned, of the child and flowers, and looking up to it. Jeannie clasped her hands with delight. I went to them, and led them round to see the other pictures,—the angels,—and the child Jesus,—and thought how much more congenial was such companionship for these little ones, and what a wrong it was to rob them of the pure, natural pleasures of childhood. They, too, ought to be asleep, dreaming of angels, instead of being in that hot room, breathing already an atmosphere poisoned for both body and soul. Dear little Jeannie! the angels soon took her to their own care.

Supper was at last announced. I looked at the clock; it was eleven. I had been anxiously waiting for my brother's carriage, for Ellen looked wearied, though Mary was in high spirits. We went to the supper room. I don't know how Mrs. Brown would have entertained Queen Victoria, but I think that

4

this supper would have done very well; and certainly, if our accounts of the simple habits of the royal children are correct, it would all have been thrown away upon them. I did not even know the names of many of the glittering confects and delicacies. I only know that they were utterly unsuitable for children, and indeed for any person at that hour. Hot oysters, chicken salad, boned turkey, hot coffee, iced lemonade, and champagne, ices and jellies, bonbons, sugared fruits and rich cakes, I looked upon with very thankless eyes. What could I do? I could not allow my children to eat them, yet it was very hard to refuse. Indeed, I could not find Mary in the crowd. Ellen and little Jeannie I had kept at my side, and I succeeded beyond my hopes in satisfying them with a few of the least unhealthy viands.

Divested of its moral aspect, it would have been a very amusing sight to see the little white-gloved gentlemen help the little impatient ladies. The largest glimpse of nature which I caught in the whole evening, was in the undisguised dissatisfaction which some little lady-faces showed on looking at their plates, and finding that they did not contain a little of every thing that was on the table, or, it might have been, of the favorite dainty which they had set their hearts upon.

At last it was all over. The supper was over; the carriage came; my children went; and my brother and I went, and we all got home again.

"Well, my little girls, have you enjoyed yourselves?" I asked.

"Ye-es ma'am, *pretty* well," said Mary. "I don't think I have, quite as well as I expected."

"And why not?"

"One thing, I think it was very mean in them,— some of the little girls laughed at my dress, and said they should not think my mother would let me go to a party in a merino dress and apron. *I* think," she added in an excited tone, " *I* think it was quite as well as being dressed up as they were. Think of little girls in silk dresses covered with lace, and white satin slippers, and white kid gloves ! *I* think it is ridiculous."

"Sad business all round," said my brother. " Here's a new evil."

"And their chains, and pins, and bracelets," added Mary. "There was one little girl there who had three bracelets on one arm, and two on the other."

I reminded her of another little girl, who had very much wished to wear her *one* bracelet. She was silent.

"And Ellen," said I, " did you enjoy it ?"

"Not so *very* much," said the little soft voice. " Only Jeannie and I had a good time, looking at the pictures. I could not dance, and some of them laughed at me, and I don't think they were very polite."

"Well, my darlings, now go to bed. I don't believe you will want to go to another such party."

"O yes I shall," said Mary, as she kissed me good night.

"I don't think I shall," said Ellen. "I should have been a great deal happier at home with you."

After the children had retired, my brother walked up and down the room in silence, for five or ten minutes. Then he spoke,—

"There is an expression in John Foster's writings, which I understand now—'*Children's parties —detestable vanities.*'" Then he walked up and down again.

"Robbed of their childhood ! Robbed of their childhood ! In such a state of society there is no childhood. These full-feathered little peacocks strut about, just like the old ones. All that has made childhood poetical and beautiful, the type of purity and simplicity, is killed out. These self-conscious, self-seeking, self-sufficient little beings, have nothing left of childhood but its ignorance. When the disciples had striven, which should be greatest, our Saviour set a little child in the midst, and said, ' Except ye humble yourselves, and become as *little children*, ye shall not enter into the kingdom of heaven.' *These* children are engaged in that very strife, in its most contemptible phase, the strife for precedence in vanity and ostentation. It is not *natural* to children. My little girls in Iowa will sit down under the tree, and dress their dolls in silks and laces, without a thought of themselves. It is a great wrong to a child, to give it the idea of possession and appropriation, as essential to enjoyment. I have heard excellent mothers say, 'What a beautiful doll that is ! I think, Susy, you must have one like it.' Why not let the child enjoy it, as belonging to another?"

" You did not hear as I did," said I, " the comments of the little girls in the dressing-room upon the dresses of others. It was pitiable. They seemed to be afraid that somebody else might be thought more tastefully, or fashionably, or expensively dressed than themselves. There were some sad exhibitions of envy and jealousy."

" And besides this," continued my brother, " it is a misfortune for anybody to have his wishes gratified too readily. I remember waiting for years for my first silver pencil, and my watch was to be the reward of a successful examination on entering college. That watch was a great thing to me—a great hope, and a great joy. We looked forward then, and thought, ' When we are old enough we shall do so and so ;' and those who *were* old enough were looked upon as a superior sort of beings. And this looking forward, this development and hope, is no small ingredient in our happiness."

"I really pitied that little boy," said I, " whose watch could be replaced so easily. He has nothing to gain."

"That is it, taking them on their own ground. They are dressed and entertained as expensively as their parents. They are in full possession of what they consider the pleasures of life. There is nothing reserved for the future. How can we expect in them humility, or deference, or reverence ? Do you suppose that many Christian parents allow their children to attend such parties ?"

"I know some that do ; and, indeed, that was one reason why I felt justified in sending mine. I remember hearing one mother lament the necessity of such things. 'It was an evil,' she said, 'but then children must become accustomed to society. They were in the world, and must learn its ways.'"

"For all that is in the world," repeated my brother emphatically, "the lusts of the flesh, the lusts of the eye, and the pride of life, is not of the Father, but of the world;" and then after a moment he added, "*unspotted from the world.*"

"How much do you suppose such a party costs —in money, I mean?"

"Mrs. L—— gave one a few weeks since, which she said cost her a hundred and fifty dollars; I supposed that was an unheard-of thing, but I presume that Mrs. Brown's expense could not have been less."

"I take it that one object in giving such a party is to show what one can afford; and let those who want such valuable information, go and see. I think that the sensible, Christian part of the community, had better keep away."

"I have had serious thoughts," continued he, "of coming to New York for a few years, mainly for the purpose of educating my children. But this evening has decided the matter. I should consider the bare knowledge, that there are children who dress, and feel, and live, in this preposterous way, as being too dear a price for a little polish and grace. I can teach my children books, and their mother can teach them both books and manners. They have good health, good minds, good feelings."

He walked up and down again, and then added:

"No, they shall stay in Iowa. They may be bears, but they shall not be monkeys."

The next morning the children were, of course, jaded, and exhausted. Their uncle proposed a walk down Broadway. They returned in high glee.

"Oh, mother," cried Ellen, "Uncle took us into a green-house, and he let us each choose a plant, to have for our own. Mary chose a rose, and I chose a jessamine. They are beautiful, so large, and all in blossom. And then Uncle bought a great many flower-seeds, and two little hoes, and two little flower-pots, and he said he was going to ask you to let us each have a garden in the back-yard."

"Yes," said he, "and I am going to petition that they may each have a dark calico frock, and a regular old-fashioned sun-bonnet, and work in their gardens an hour every morning."

"I should rejoice to have them work three," I replied.

"Well, now, what did you see down Broadway?" asked their mother.

"I saw a little boy on a pony," said Mary.

"I saw a poor woman," said Ellen; "she was

sitting on a step with two little babies, and they were asleep, and Uncle let us give the woman a shilling.   And we saw a lady walking with the dearest little dog, tied to a string that she held in her hand."

"We saw a little calf," said Mary, "in one of the side streets; it was following its mother, and going to be killed, I suppose.   It was too bad."

"There, you may go.   Now, sister," he added, earnestly, after they had left the room, "there is nature left in your children.   You may think I am too serious, but I can think only of this verse—'Take heed that ye offend not one of these little ones; for I say unto you that in heaven their angels do always behold the face of my Father which is in heaven.'"

MAYING AT SPRINGDALE.

SPRINGDALE, *May* 10, 1856.

MY DEAR COUSIN:

I THANK you for your letter which gave me an account of your May-day morning. We all laughed heartily about it, though I do not believe that you felt much like laughing at the time. I hope that before now you have a bed to sleep on, and a place for your trunk where it can be opened, and some plates and cups and saucers, and a clear space large enough for your dining-table. It seems strange to think of your moving so often, because I have lived

in the same house all my life, and father was born
here too. I am glad that you have that dear little
room for your own. I should love to make you a
visit in it. Father told Minnie that uncle had built
a house so convenient, that it only needed to be
wound up once a week like a clock, and then it
would "go" of itself. But Minnie did not seem
quite to believe in such a wonder. Well, I hope that
you will soon be "settled," and be very happy in
your new home, and never move again, till you come
to live in Springdale.

Now, I must tell you how *I* spent May-day, or a
part of it. It was Tuesday, you know. On Monday,
Mr. Benson, our teacher, happened to be sick, which,
of course, we were very sorry for, although it was
very convenient for us, as it gave us more time to
carry out our plans. In the afternoon, Sophia Wells,
Julia Herbert and myself, the "three inseparables,"

as the other girls call us, had some very important
business, which was to take a walk and gather
flowers, to make bouquets for May morning. We
went up Oak-hill, which, you remember, is beyond
Mr. Herbert's, on the way to Greenville.

It was a beautiful day, the mildest we had had.
We were on the south side of the hill, where the air
was warm and soft, and the bright green grass, and
the budding trees, and the fresh leaves springing up
among the dark mosses and around the old roots, all
gave us the delicious, indescribable feeling of the
return of Spring. We sat down for a while on a
log, for we could do nothing but enjoy ourselves.
You would have laughed to hear our exclamations,
every thing was so beautiful. We looked down on
the meadows, clothed in their soft Spring colors, and
on the blue river winding through them, and on the
little clumps of trees with their different tints, and

on the village with its white spires and pretty houses, and to the far-off mountains, beautiful in the rosy and violet mist, and up to the blue sky, with its clouds of fleece and silver, it was all so lovely!

I should think that we sat an hour on that old log, pointing out to each other one beauty after another, and singing for very gladness. At last we proceeded to business, the important business of gathering flowers. I had with me the tin box which we have carried so often, and Julia and Sophia brought baskets. We had not many wild flowers in blossom so early, in spite of the poets; but we found violets, and hepaticas, and anemonies, and May flowers, (what you call the trailing arbutus,) and my favorite of all wild flowers, that delicate straw-colored bell, the uvularia. It is mamma's favorite too, and, I dare say, that is the reason why it is mine.

Gathering Flowers.

So we wandered about, singing and gathering flowers. The May flowers are very beautiful on that hill, large, deep-colored and fragrant. We gathered, a great many. I filled my box with anemonies and violets and uvularias, because they were most likely to wither; and the other girls took some too, for my box would not hold all we wanted; and they filled up their baskets with May flowers and every thing else they could find. At last, when we had gathered as many as we could carry, and were pretty tired, too, we trotted down the hill, and went home through the back street, so as not to be seen, and through our orchard, in at the back door. Julia and Sophia staid to tea, and in the evening, with mamma's help, we arranged our bouquets. I think that mamma enjoyed it as much as we did.

The first thing was to decide to whom we would give them. We had flowers enough, we thought,

5

for eight or ten bouquets, so we each chose two persons. Sophia chose Dr. Lawrence, our minister, and Miss Anna Story, who was to be married on Wednesday. Julia chose Mr. Benson and Madame Erskine. You remember what a beautiful old lady she is. I chose Mrs. Everett, who is sick, and is very fond of flowers, and little May Clifford, who was just a year old on May day. Then we wanted mamma to choose two, but she said she would only select one, and that was—who do you think? Aunt Sally Brown, the old woman who has been sick so long in the little brown house near the Post office.

The next thing was to decide which flowers were most suitable for each person, then the color of the ribbons, and lastly the mottoes. But I will not tell you how we arranged all these important points, only that we did arrange them at last, and made our bouquets, and left them for the night in a large tin

pan filled with water, and left the ribbons and mottoes ready to be tied on in the morning, when Sophia
and Julia were to come for me.

I hope they slept as soundly as I did. I sprang
up the moment that Betty called me, at four o'clock,
with a feeling that something important was to be
done, though, I confess, it did seem rather early. I
was not quite dressed when the girls came. We tied
up the bouquets as quickly as possible, and before five
started on our expedition. And it was such a beautiful morning that we pitied everybody who was not
up and enjoying it. The eastern sky was streaked
with gold and crimson. The birds were singing
everywhere, and all nature seemed rejoicing. I
thought of you, asleep in your crowded, noisy city,
and longed to have you with me. But I must tell
you about our bouquets, and what we did with
them.

We came first to Mrs. Everett's. We opened
the gate carefully, and hung her bouquet on the
knob of the door-bell. It was made of violets and
uvularias, and tied with green ribbon. I think it
was one of the prettiest, so delicate and graceful.
The motto was from Mary Howitt :

" Then wherefore, wherefore were they made,
   All dyed in rainbow light,
   Growing in sunshine and in shade,
   Upspringing day and night ?—
   Springing in deserts lone and wild,
   And on the mountains high,
   And in the silent wilderness
   Where no man passes by
   To whisper hope, to comfort man,
   Whene'er his faith is dim,
   For who so careth for the flowers
   Will much more care for him."

We next left Mr. Benson's, with his name on it,

hanging on the door of his boarding-house. It was very large, made of all the different kinds of flowers, and tied with pink. The motto was from Milton. He is always quoting Milton to us.

> " Now the bright morning star, day's harbinger,
>   Comes dancing from the east, and brings with her
>   The flowery May, who from her green lap throws
>   The yellow cowslip and the pale primrose."

Then we left the little baby May's. You will guess what it was made of. May flowers only, fresh and rosy and fragrant, and tied with blue ribbon. The motto was this : " For the May blossom. Sweets for the sweet."

The next house was Madame Erskine's. Her bouquet was beautiful, of evergreens mingled with the flowers, and tied with green. The motto was from one of her favorite poems, Wordsworth's ode, which I had read to her a few days before :

" Thanks to the human heart by which we live,
    Thanks to its tenderness, its hopes and fears,
    To me the meanest flower that blows can give
    Thoughts which do often lie too deep for tears."

We came then to Aunt Sally's. Her bouquet was very pretty, and tied with scarlet. Mamma arranged it, and selected the motto, for she said that no words would sound to Aunt Sally so sweet as these :

" Wherefore, if God so clothe the grass of the field, which to-day is, and to-morrow is cast in the oven, will he not much more clothe you, oh ye of little faith ?"

The bride came next. The bouquet was of anemonies, May flowers and sprigs of myrtle, and tied with white satin ribbon. The motto was from Mrs. Hemans :

" Bring flowers, bright flowers for the bride to wear ;
  They were born to blush in her shining hair.
  She is leaving the home of her childhood's mirth,
  She has bid farewell to her father's hearth.
  Her place is now by another's side,
  Bring flowers for the locks of the fair young bride."

Our last call was at the parsonage, and we left the bouquet, hanging from the door-knob by its blue ribbon. It was made of all the varieties of flowers, with green sprigs of the arbor vitæ, the " tree of life." The motto was from Horace Smith's "Hymn to the Flowers :"

" ' Neath cloistered boughs each floral bell that swingeth,
  And tolls its perfume on the passing air,
  Makes Sabbath in the fields, and ever ringeth
  A call to prayer."

Our work was then done, and we went home as

quickly as possible, so that nobody should see the fairies who had brought their gifts.

I had still something to do. I had selected the evening before some of my most beautiful uvularias, and kept them in water, and now I made them into a bouquet, and tied them with a blue ribbon. They looked lovely, The motto, too, I liked,—from Keble's Christian Year :

"So have I seen, in spring's bewitching hour,
   When the glad earth is offering all her best,
   Some gentle maid bend o'er a cherished flower,
   And wish it worthier on a parent's heart to rest."

I went softly and hung it on the handle of my mother's door.

Now, I have made a long story, but I thought you would like to know all about it. How I wish that you lived here ! I begin to count the weeks before your coming—only six now. Papa has had a flower-bed made for you, next to mine, and I have planted a good many seeds. I hope that they will all be up and growing finely when you come.

Please give my love to Uncle and Aunt, and accept a great deal yourself from

Your ever affectionate cousin,

CORNELIA L.

P. S.—Next Wednesday is my birth-day. Only think! I shall be fifteen years old.

THE FOURTH OF JULY.

WHAT a beautiful day that was! Not beautiful in the morning, which was dull and foggy; but that was not discouraging, since no one in those days was so unpatriotic as to suppose that it could rain on the Fourth of July. It certainly did not rain on that day. On the contrary, the sun burst forth before nine o'clock, and gave his morning salutation to the pretty village of A———, which had, hours before, received the greetings of the bells of the two churches and the Academy, and of all the cannon which could be mustered, amounting to two. How gloriously that sun illumined first the fog, and then the hills, and trees, and fresh, green fields! How softly through the north window came in that morning breeze, fragrant from the curtain of sweetbriar and syringa!

At that hour there was scarcely a sound to be heard through the village. The sunrise demonstrations of bells and cannon had been succeeded by an hour or two of shouts and cracker explosions upon the common; but now the inhabitants, old and young, were quietly in-doors, preparing for the celebration in the old church. There was to be an Oration by Judge Lane, and a Poem by the distinguished Mr. Graham from Boston, and the Declaration of Independence was to be read by Dr. Reynolds. For this, grey-headed men were putting on their Sunday clothes, and their wives and daughters hurrying through their preparations for a cold dinner on their return, and then arraying themselves in their best. For this, little boys were putting on clean shirts, and well-brushed shoes, and white pantaloons, some even fastening roses in the button-holes of their jackets. For this, little girls were carefully donning, for the first time that summer, their smooth white dresses, and pink or blue sashes, and tying the gipsey hats, trimmed with wreaths of fragrant roses, over their sunny curls. For this, Dr. Reynolds was nervously walking up and down his little parlor, repeating slowly and emphatically, " certain inalienable rights—life, liberty, and the pursuit of happiness." For this, Judge Lane was seated at his library table, carefully reading, and pencilling here and there the pages of a very, very thick pile of manuscript.

But, not for this, were a dozen or more of the selectest girls of the village making their busy preparations. Not to grace the galleries of the village church were those white muslins and gay ribbons laid out, and those bright flowers twined into wreaths, and gathered into bouquets. No, indeed! those patriotic young ladies were to have a celebration of their own,—an Oration, and a Poem, and an Ode, and a feast, all in a pretty bower in the woods. Nobody was to know any thing about it; nobody, at least, but their mothers, whose consent and assistance were rather important in the preparations for the table ; and nobody else but their brothers, whose skill and strong arms were likewise necessary for the building of the bower, and the arrangement of the said table. With these exceptions, nobody was to know "any thing" about it. In vain had brothers pleaded. Ned White would give any thing to hear Mary Stone's Oration, and Harry Stevens had a great mind to say that he would not help at all, if he could not hear the Poem, and Sam Williams said that some of the Academy boys would never get over it, if it "came off" without their knowledge. But the sisters were inexorable. "No, it would spoil the whole if any body but themselves should be there. Nobody should know a word about it, and, above all things, no Academy boys!" If the brothers would be very good, they should come in for a share of the feast after the literary performances were over; but this was all the grace granted to the most urgent entreaties.

So the boys made the best of the matter, and very obligingly built the bower, and a very pretty one it was. There was a thick, extensive wood, commencing half a mile from the village; and in this wood, on a smooth green spot, overshadowed by a large oak, they had planted two rows of young ash trees, and tied their branches together at the top. Outside of these, fir trees were ranged at intervals, one also standing at each side of the entrance. Wreaths made of oak leaves were hung within, looped up, as the hour approached, by bouquets of roses. At the end farthest from the entrance was an elevated seat, and benches were placed along the two sides. The centre of the bower was occupied by a long table, covered with snowy damask, brilliant with glass and silver, gay with wreaths and vases of flowers, and lighted up with sunbeams, flickering through shadows of waving boughs. In the centre of the table was a large vase, containing a magnificent bouquet composed entirely of white lilies and elder blossoms. Nor must the tempting delicacies with which it was loaded be unmentioned,—cakes, tarts, and jellies, and strawberries and cream. The "boys" had been successful in privately conveying thither, not only the table and its contents, but also the young girls who had so tastefully adorned it.

And now, when the hour arrived, taking advantage of the universal patriotic feeling, which collected all the villagers either in the church, or on the piazza of the "Tontine," where the public dinner was to be served, our white-robed, merry band of girls proceeded to their pretty bower, where two of their number were already keeping guard over their secret treasures.

Many were the exclamations of delight as they entered, and surveyed the scene, and a spectator would have found fresh food for admiration in these youthful, happy occupants of the bower—the fairies of the fairy land. They were sixteen in number, all in white dresses, decorated with roses and other flowers of the season, in wreaths, and sprigs, and bouquets, according to their various fancies. Fresh and bright as the flowers were the young faces, the sparkling eyes, and glowing cheeks.

Having entered and fairly taken possession of their bower, there was a pause in the merry tones, for they really did not know what to do first. Somebody proposed choosing a queen, and a queen was chosen, forgetting that the occasion of their celebration was their independence of crowned heads. Mary Ellis was the chosen one, and was led to the raised seat at the end of the bower. One of the girls snatched from the table a beautiful wreath of roses and elder-blossoms, and placed it on her head. Her usually pale face was radiant with happy blushes, and illumined at times with a sunbeam, which seemed lovingly to seek it again and again. At length, when all were seated, she rose, and, with embarrassed dignity, announced the order of exercises—The Declaration of Independence to be read by Miss Jane Edwards, an Oration by Miss Mary Stone, a Poem by Miss Alice Ste-

6

phens, and, in conclusion, an original Ode was to be sung.

As the queen took her seat, all eyes turned to Jane Edwards, who, blushingly, and with down-cast look, took her station at the end of the table, and, in defiance of all etiquette, with her back to the queen. She commenced in a low tone, but her courage rose as she proceeded, till she was enabled to recount the injuries her country had received from its oppressors with as much indignant energy as the gentleman-reader manifested in the village church. She finished and took her seat, with the appearance of being very glad that her part was over.

Then came the Oration. Mary Stone rose, and took her post with a firm step, erect head, and the air of one who did every thing in an independent, fearless way. She had a good honest face, which every body loved to look at, and it never was more attractive than now, when, slightly flushed, and all in earnest, she delivered her patriotic speech. She considered this country as the greatest which the sun shone upon. "Assyria, Greece, Rome, Carthage, where are they? Never should that question be asked of America. In what other country under heaven could such a sight be seen as this—young girls assembled, out of pure patriotism, to celebrate the anniversary of their country's independence?" It was too bad, but there were some roguish smiles cast at this moment upon the well-spread table, unperceived however by the eloquent Orator, who went on, her patriotism warming at every sentence, till she finished with an earnest appeal to her companions to prove themselves worthy citizens, daughters, wives and mothers in this glorious republic. She took her seat amid great applause.

Some moments elapsed before the enthusiasm of

the audience had subsided sufficiently to attend to
the Poem. At length the Poet was called for, and
Alice Stephens, all in trepidation, stood at the head
of the table. She was a sensitive, retiring girl,
shrinking from censure as much as she craved ap-
probation. Evidently making a great effort, with a
faltering voice, she commenced :

> " While older people celebrate this day,
>   When on our country first shone freedom's ray,
>   While they rejoice that this land is their own,
>   The land where despotism was never known,
>   The land where every heart is brave and free,
>   The land of Washington and Liberty,
>   Shall we, though young, refuse their names to bless
>   Who purchased with their blood our happiness ?
>   Shall we——"

Here her trembling voice gave out entirely, and
Alice first giggled, and then cried, and then sat

down, and covered her face with her pocket hand-
kerchief. In vain did her companions protest and
beg. In vain did the queen leave her throne to
comfort and encourage the mortified girl. It was
all over with the poem.

Seeing that it was all over, the queen as soon as
possible diverted the attention of the audience by
announcing the Ode. This performance, which like
the Poem was more remarkable for patriotism than
originality and some other qualities, was composed
by Sophia Clinton. The whole group rose to sing
it, and it certainly sounded better than even thê
author anticipated ; for it was sung, not only by the
pleasant voices of the young girls, as was expected,
but also by the most unexpected addition of a fine
tenor and bass from the tree above. The girls
looked at each other in consternation, but not a
glance was turned upward, not a voice stopped or

faltered, though the faces looked unutterable things. Still they sang on, and still those voices above sang too, as if it was all planned, and just what was expected.

When the singing was over, then indeed those sweet voices took another tune; and if those " nuisances," those " mean fellows," those " interlopers," those " disgraceful creatures," had heard, as they could not well help hearing, the flattering epithets that were showered upon them, they must have wished themselves on the lowest branches of that oak tree.   Then the young ladies proceeded to speak in different phrases of their invited guests, who must have seemed very enviable beings to the neglected intruders. These fortunate persons at length arrived, and the singers on the tree-top had probably the satisfaction of looking down upon the merry company partaking of the feast of good things.

Years have passed since that happy day. That band of merry school-girls is widely scattered. The next year saw the queen, then so radiant in her wreath of lilies, transplanted to a brighter summer and a more congenial soil. The passing years have taken one after another. Some have daughters more than their own changed selves resembling the girls whose laugh and song resounded within that bower. As for the trespassers in the oak tree, it never was known positively who they were, but probably a certain New England Judge, and a certain New York clergyman, could tell as much as any body about the matter.

THE SEA-SIDE.

"WE are going to the sea-side, Fanny! We are going to the sea-side!" shouted Charles Weston, rushing into the room, where his sister was learning her French lesson. "When? Where? How do you know?" "Oh, father and mother have it all planned. They mean to go next Thursday, and stay three or four weeks. Father has engaged rooms in a nice farm-house, at H———. Is not it grand?" "I am *so* glad," exclaimed Fanny, who hastened at once to headquarters, for confirmation of the joyful news. It was all true. They were to go to the sea-side, and next Thursday, too—so soon!

The intervening days passed quickly, in preparations for the great event. In the first place, Fanny, being an orderly young lady, arranged her drawers and book-case, closet and play-room. She selected a few favorite books, to take with her, among which were her French Picciola, and Abbott's History of Marie Antoinette; for she did not intend to be idle, even at the sea-side. Then, out of her numerous family of dolls, she decided that Jenny Lind and Victoria should go with her, because Jenny's face was paler than dolls' faces are wont to be, and Victoria's wardrobe was in a condition to do her credit. So Cinderella, and Topsey, and Rose, and the dear little crying baby, Lilly, were attired in their best, and put to bed in a drawer, with the expectation that they would sleep over the whole excursion, and wake up when Fanny returned, just as if nothing had happened, but a nice little nap.

Fanny, under her mother's direction, selected the dresses which she was to take. These were, for the most part, plain, substantial ginghams and prints, with two or three of a better sort, for Sundays and special occasions. She must have a bathing dress, and a sun-bonnet, besides her bloomer. By her mother's advice, she put in her trunk an old ledger of her father's, some thick letter-paper, and a quantity of soft old muslin, the use of which articles she was yet to learn.

Master Charles, in the mean time, selected books, English and Latin, which went into his trunk, in company with the stoutest and worst-looking clothes he could muster; for he intended to " do the thing thoroughly," and "make a regular sailor."

Thursday came at last. Charles and Fanny were up at sunrise. Alas, it was a drizzly, uncomfortable morning, and although it was the middle of July, the raw air suggested warm clothing. Fanny's warm plaid shawl was at the bottom of her trunk, and she could not well do without it. However, there was time enough to unpack and take it out. "Now, my dear Fanny," said Charles, gravely, "let me give you one piece of advice, which will be of service all your life long. *Never put any thing at the bottom of your trunk.* If you do, you will be sure to want it, whatever it is." Fanny laughed, and told him she wished he would pack it for her after that fashion.

An early breakfast was eaten, and at half-past seven the carriage was at the door, to convey the travellers to the railroad station. Mrs. Weston gave various last charges to the servants, who were to remain, about "locking up at night," being "careful about matches," "not letting in suspicious people," &c. &c., which Charles, in his impatience, thought quite unnecessary, as there was not a more careful and trusty person in the world than old Sarah, to say nothing of John. But the last words were said, the trunks and carpet-bags all adjusted to the satisfaction of the driver, the door closed, the last lingering though rather triumphant looks given to the home so dear, yet so willingly left, and the travellers were on their way.

It was late in the afternoon when they reached H——. The "cloudy morning" had "turned out a fine day," and the July sun made no less refreshing than beautiful the glimpses of ocean, which now, on their road, became more frequent and more extended. H— was in itself a place of peculiar beauty. The house of Mr. Ward stood on a high bluff, called from its shape the Round Rock; it commanded a wide view of the open sea in front, and of a fine beach, which stretched on both sides, though interrupted by the bluff. This beach extended on the

The Sea Side.

right, round a cove, for two or three miles, when it was terminated by another bluff, called the South Rock, on which was built a large hotel, a favorite resort in summer of the inhabitants of the neighboring villages. At the left, or northeast of Mr. Ward's house, the beach stretched for half a mile, till it was terminated by a promontory, (which at high tide was an island,) thickly wooded with evergreens. Its sides were formed of broken rock, forming numerous basins for the tide, and deposits for shells and sea-weeds. At its extremity rude seats were arranged under the trees, and, on a warm afternoon, a more delightful spot could hardly be found, or thought of. Here, in addition to the view from Round Rock, was to be seen a varied line of coast to the northward, and a pretty group of wooded islands, called the Deer Islands. Nearly opposite the South Rock, a mile out at sea, on a rock, which was the termination of a dangerous ledge, stood a light-house. Others, at various distances, could, on a clear day, be distinctly seen. Back of Mr. Ward's house, a few rods distant, was his farm, a small part of which was devoted to vegetables, while the greater portion was salt meadow-land, covered with rich grass. Half a mile back was the pretty village of H——, whose white and slender church-spire was visible for miles around.

To this pleasant place our travellers came, at the close of their day's journey. The July sun sent its slant rays over the landscape, and bathed the broad ocean in glory. The children could not restrain their delight in the beauty of the scene, which increased at every step of their approach. " Look here, Fanny !" " Do see this, Charles." " Mother, was there ever any thing more beautiful !" They drove at last through Mr. Ward's land, to his house, near the edge of the

Round Rock, and stopped at the open door. If any thing had been wanting to complete the satisfaction of our travellers, their kind reception by Mr. and Mrs. Ward, the neat and pleasant rooms, and plentiful, well-arranged table, must have supplied it.

After the refreshments of cold water, combs and brushes, and a good supper, Charles and Fanny walked out to survey this region of delights. Nothing escaped their admiring eyes. The sun was setting, and the broad ocean was in a golden glow. Never was such verdure as on those salt meadows, never such "light on sea or land," never such a sky, tinted and radiant with beauty and glory. They seated themselves at last upon the door-step, and watched the varying tints, the deepening shades, and, as Charles expressed it, "the sober look, which came, by degrees, over the face of old Neptune." Then the first pale star peeped out, and soon another. The white sails, which, a few moments before, were radiant as they caught the sunlight, could now hardly be distinguished from the dark water. The sky faded, the shadows blackened, the fir grove on the promontory looked dark and gloomy. " Look !' cried Fanny, pointing to the light-house, whose revolving light, like a great red star, suddenly shone in the distance. In a minute it vanished, in another it returned, and they watched it long, with unabated interest. Fainter lights gleamed from various points. The white surf came toward them with its majestic tread, breaking in playful ripples upon the beach, but now its glittering beauty was gone, and they listened rather than looked, for until now, they had scarcely noticed the grandeur of its tone. The fresh sea-air gave them energy and exhilaration. They seemed to be almost in an enchanted region. Every sense drank in delight.

Mrs. Weston at length reminded them of their long journey, and of the new pleasures which the morrow was to bring. So they left the "dear old ocean," as reluctantly as if it had been a dear old friend, and after their evening prayers they were soon asleep in their nice little beds. Nor were their prayers hurried, or unfelt; for they loved to think of all this grandeur, and all this enjoyment, as coming from their heavenly Father, whom they loved, and whom they wished to serve. How could they forget Him there, in the midst of his great works, and the beauty which He had made!

The morning brought new enjoyment. Charles and Fanny walked on the beach, and there took off their shoes and stockings, and ventured to the water's edge, in safe defiance of the rippling tide. " See, the ocean is coming to play with me!" cried Fanny in delight. Then, as the waves receded, they picked

7

up the waifs of delicate sea-weeds and pretty shells, and bounded forward, hand-in-hand, to be ready for the next approach. They filled their little baskets with their treasures, and at last went up to the house with them, for they had a new pleasure in prospect, no less an one than bathing in the surf.

So they accoutred themselves, Mrs. Weston and Charles and Fanny, in the strange garments called bathing-dresses. If they had met any body in Broadway in such attire, they would have wondered whether it was a Chinese, or a Patagonian, or a South Sea Islander, or perhaps the man in the moon.

Now, if any of my little readers do not know the delight of sea-bathing, there is no use in trying to describe it. The fresh pure air, the exhilaration, dancing in the water, bounding with the bounding waves, plunging into the surf, waiting for one wave, and then another and another, till some unexpected but not unwelcome one comes pouring over you, head and all, and you hardly know what *has* come, or indeed, any thing at all, except that you are lost in a great, sweeping, dashing, roaring, overwhelming something, and you must keep still till it is gone. It would be very dangerous for young people to learn this pleasure by themselves, but learned in the proper way, that is, in company with their elders, it is very delightful. Charles and Fanny loved the ocean more, the more they knew of it. If it was hard for them to stop looking at it the evening before, it was still harder to stop feeling it now; but at last they emerged, and ran in high glee to the little bathing-houses, where they dressed themselves, and went very merry, and very hungry to the house. In the afternoon they read, and the evening was spent like the previous one.

The next day at low tide they walked, with

their parents, to the end of the wooded promontory, and sat for a long time watching the water, and the sails, and casting longing looks to the pretty Deer Islands. They climbed down the rocks, and filled their baskets with new varieties of sea-weeds. When they returned, behold the tide was rising : they had staid too long ! But they must make the best of it. The children took off their shoes and stockings, and waded through the rising water, stepping on the smooth stones, and, on the whole, were very glad of the adventure.

The next day Mr. Ward took them, in his nice double-waggon, with two horses, along the beautiful beach, to the South Rock, and back again.

But Charles' greatest desire was yet to be gratified. So, on the fourth day, there was a fishing excursion. Mr. Ward had a sail-boat, " The Gipsey," and he and his son took the management of it, and two other gentlemen who were also boarding at Mr. Ward's, accompanied them. The day was fine, and a brisk breeze added to the excitement of the sail. Fanny was a little timid at first, but her courage gradually rose, till she enjoyed the trip greatly. She put out her hand to play with the water, and bounded with the motion of the boat, and, before they were back to land, she felt quite like an old sailor. As for Charles, he began to understand the sailor's love for the grand old sea. The ocean is full of charms to a boy. There is to him a wild exulting freedom in riding on its boundless bosom, drinking in its fresh exhilarating air, feeling and braving its power, guiding his tiny boat securely over its waves, moving with its motion, till he seems to become part of it, and communing, as it were, with the great heart of nature. No wonder that boys love it!

Never had they tasted such delicious mackerel as Mrs. Ward broiled for their dinner on their return. Mrs. Weston said she had just learned the meaning of the recipe of Mrs. Glass, "First *catch* the hare."

So the days passed, only too quickly. The mornings were given to bathing and various excursions, and the afternoons to reading and quiet employments. At the end of a fortnight, there was a great storm. Charles and Fanny sat for hours at the windows, watching the tossing, tumultuous waves, and listening to their roar. "This would be a good day for pressing your sea-weeds, Fanny," said the mother. "So it would! Thank you, mother. Will you show me how?" "Certainly, dear. Bring your book, and muslin and paper, and we will go to work."

Fanny obeyed. Charles opened a large table, and put upon it two basins of water, in one of which the sea-weeds were soaking. Mrs. Weston selected one, and put it in the clean water in the other basin. Then she slipped a piece of rather thick white paper under it, and, with a large needle, arranged the branches and delicate fibres, clipping here, and adding there, according to her taste. She kept it just wet enough to move it readily on the paper, yet not too wet, lest the water should disarrange her work. Then she lifted the paper very carefully out of the water, and laid it, with the sea-weed uppermost, on a bit of smooth muslin which was lying ready on an open page of the old ledger. She then covered the sea-weed with another smooth piece of muslin, taking care not to disarrange any part of it. So she, and Fanny, and Charles prepared one after another, laying them in different parts of the book. Mrs. Weston carefully closed the book, and, for want of a better weight, placed it under one of the posts of the bed. There it remained until morning, when they carefully removed the pieces of muslin, and put dry ones in their stead, and placed the book again under the bed-post. The next day they took out the papers, with the mosses adhering to them, more beautiful and delicate than paintings. Mrs. Weston taught Fanny to arrange the different varieties together, in wreaths and bouquets, some of which were very tasteful and elegant. Fanny still preserves a book full of them.

After her return home, a kind lady taught her to make tiny baskets, or half-baskets, of straw attached to card-board, and to fill them with bouquets of the more delicate sea-weeds, interspersed with the fine wood-mosses, kept in place by being gummed to the card-board. Out of the black, bead-like excrescences on the coarse sea-weed, Fanny learned to make bracelets and rings, by selecting those of the same size and shape, nicely cutting off the ends, and stringing them (for they are hollow) on a black elastic cord. The little shells, too, were not suffered to lie useless, but were arranged and gummed on card-board, for various ornamental purposes. If you will call at Mrs. Weston's, in Tenth street, I do not doubt that Fanny will be very glad to show them to you, and to tell you many more pleasant things about her month at the sea-side.

MARY MELVILLE'S BIRTH-DAY.

"How different it is from what I expected! I thought that father and mother would be back, and that we should have been in our own dear home again. Every morning for the last week I have thought that they would surely be here before night. It seems so long to wait! It is so hard to be patient, but I must try. Yes, and I *will* try, for mother's sake."

So thought Mary Melville, on the morning of the day when she was ten years old. She sat at the window, with her head resting on her hand, so much absorbed in her own feelings that she did not notice the entrance of her aunt, until she felt an arm around her neck.

Mrs. Duncan had enough of both kindness and imagination to make her a ready sympathizer. She said, with her sweet smile and gentle voice, " I came to give my little Mary a birth-day-kiss. Not quite so good as mother's, but a very loving one."

" Oh, Aunt Alice," said Mary, " I did *so* hope that father and mother would be here to-day. But you are *next best* to them," she added, smiling through her tears, and returning her aunt's kiss.

" We all hoped that they would be here, my darling. But God has ordered it otherwise. He could easily have brought them, if He had chosen."

" What do you think is the reason that they have not come? Do you think they are safe?"

asked Mary in a low voice, as if afraid to give utterance to her fears.

"There is not the slightest reason for anxiety, and will not be if they do not come for a week yet. Sailing packets are very irregular."

Mary heaved a deep sigh.

"It is hard, I know, my darling, to bear such a disappointment; this long waiting is hard work for older people. But it is our Heavenly Father who directs every thing, and we must trust Him when his ways are not our ways. You will try to be patient and cheerful, will you not?"

Mary's reply was a kiss, and a gentle loving look.

"Do you think mother remembers that this is my birth-day?" she asked, after a pause.

"I am sure of it, dear; and here is somebody to tell you so," replied her aunt, giving her a small parcel which she had not perceived before.

Mary opened it, and discovered a beautiful Bible, with her name upon the cover.

"How did this come? How could mother send it?"

"The last letter which we received from her contained a request that I would have it ready for you, as she feared that they might not be here to-day."

"Dear, good mother!" exclaimed Mary, kissing the Bible, "and dear, good Aunty," kissing her aunt. "You have chosen the very kind I like best, with such nice large print, and clasps, and the cover so plain and so handsome, too. *Thank* you, dear Aunty."

"Now it is almost breakfast time, and I will leave you till then. Will you not select one verse to learn this morning?"

"Where is that verse, 'The Lord is good, a

stronghold in the day of trouble. He honoreth them that trust in Him?'"

Her aunt found it for her, and, tenderly kissing her, left the room. Mary felt very calm and happy. Again and again she kissed her beautiful Bible, which seemed to be almost a part of her dear mother, and her heart was full of the comforts of the sweet verse she had selected. At length she prepared to go to the breakfast room.

"I am afraid the boys will see that I have been crying," she thought, "and Horace will laugh at me." But, conquering her repugnance, she went down stairs, and met her cousins with a smiling face.

Horace was at home in his college vacation. He was in his Sophomore year, and felt very patronizing toward his little cousin.

"What an X-*ten*-sive young lady we have here," he exclaimed, putting his hand on her head, as she passed him.

Mary tried very hard to smile at the joke, and succeeded just poorly enough to make Horace doubt whether she understood it.

Her uncle came toward her, and smilingly gave her ten kisses, which did not make her smiles come any more readily; at least tears came with them. Her uncle lifted her gently to her seat at the table. "Be careful," he said, "for you have a hard cushion."

Mary looked to see it, and beheld a beautiful rose-wood writing-desk, with a silver plate on the top.

"Just look at the outside now," said her uncle, "and leave the inside till after breakfast."

The words on the plate were, "Mary Melville." She threw her arms around her uncle's neck and kissed him, without saying a word, but her face was radiant with delight.

"What have you there, Bridget?" asked Mrs.

Duncan, as the girl smilingly placed a covered plate before Mary.

"It is Peggy's present to Miss Mary, ma'am."

Mary took off the cover and counted ten little cakes, delicate and tempting as cakes could be. "Oh thank her! thank you all!" she exclaimed.

After breakfast came prayers, in which Mary was remembered in a way which made the tears come again. Afterward her uncle came to her and said, "Now we will see the inside of this wonderful desk."

He opened it, and disclosed the neat lining, and the conveniences with which it was furnished,—letter paper, and note paper, and envelopes, all stamped "M. M.," and sealing-wax, and an agate seal, and a penknife, and ever so many other things. Mary did not know what to do or say to let her uncle know how much she thanked him, but he saw how happy she was.

"This pretty knife is from Horace, and the paper knife from William, and the gold pen from your aunt." Mary looked up smilingly and said, "Thank you."

She spent almost all the forenoon in admiring the desk, and in arranging and re-arranging its contents.

"I will write a note to mother," she thought at last. "No, the first use I make of the things must be to write a note to uncle, to tell him how much I thank him, and then I will write to mother." So she wrote:

"My dear Uncle,—

"I thank you for my beautiful writing-desk. I thank you for the outside and for the inside. I thank you for the big paper, and for the little paper, and for the envelopes, and for the sealing-wax, and

8

for the pens, and for the pencils, and for all the other things.   And I thank Aunt for the gold pen, and Horace for the pearl penknife, and Willy for the ivory paper-folder.   I thank you all with all my heart.   " Your affectionate little

" MARY.'

She then folded the note with the paper-knife, and put it in one of her neat envelopes, sealed it, and stamped · the wax with the pretty agate seal, engraved with a flying dove, and felt very proud and happy all the while.

She next wrote a note to her mother, which I shall not copy, but which said how very kind every body was to her, and how very, very much she longed to see her own dear father and mother, but that she would try to be patient and happy till God should bring them back.

" I am very glad that your desk gives you so

much pleasure," said her aunt, after Mary had sealed and directed her note.

"I don't think that any thing else could have given me so much—I mean besides father's and mother's coming. Only it seems *too much* to have all these and my Bible too."

Mary was not one of those pampered children, to whom valuable presents are an every-day occurrence, and with whom gratitude given does not keep pace with benefits received. Her mother had taken great care to teach her that our happiness does not come from gifts, or from love, or from any thing which we can receive from others, but only from the feelings which go out of our own hearts. Her aunt did not forget this; but she knew, too, that there was little danger that Mary would not give back loving and thankful feelings, more precious than any thing which could be given her. For Mary was not one of those who are always craving gifts and attentions, admiration and love, but was rather always giving them out of her free and loving heart, as the sun gives out its beams. She was not one of the " receivers," who, like the whirlpool, seek to draw every thing within their reach into their own unsatisfied grasp, from which nothing returns. She was rather like the calm lake, which seems almost to lose its own being in the beautiful things of earth and heaven pictured in its loving breast.

Dinner came at five o'clock, after a pleasant afternoon drive. After dinner they all sat awhile talking, without lights, except from the cheerful fire. At length Mr. Duncan was called away on business.

" Suppose, Horace, you should read to us the story you translated yesterday," said Mrs. Duncan. " I think that Mary would enjoy it."

The gas was lighted, and Horace read

THE FABLE OF THE APE.

[Translated from the German, by HORACE DUNCAN, Esq.]

When the beasts left Paradise, after the fall of man, and became his enemies, the wildest and wickedest of them, the lion, the tiger, the wolf, the bear, and many others went together into the woods and deserts, and lived by robbery and murder, persecuting and devouring the weaker animals.

The greater part of these weaker ones then fled to the farthest hiding-place, and lived in continual fear and dread. As for example, the deer, the hare, and the roe; but the gentler and more friendly animals, the oxen, the sheep, and dogs, and many others, would gladly again have had a master, who would be kind to them, and take care of them as man had done.

They held for that purpose a great council, and

determined at last to choose the ape, because he was most like man, for he had a very grave and wise face, walked upright on two legs, and was provided with hands, with which he could conveniently handle things.

In order that he might first be well fitted for so high an office, they sent him on a certain time into the neighborhood of man, so that he could learn various arts, and then make them known to the beasts.

The ape was ready for that at once, and went to the place where Adam and Eve lived with their children. There he seated himself in an apple-tree, and observed what they did. Whoever saw him sitting there, with his important mien, must have thought, "if he does not learn it nobody can."

The first week, it was his task to notice how men built their huts; for the beasts, too, wanted to be protected from the bad weather.

He saw, from his tree, how Adam took an axe, and struck with it against the trees, till they fell; how he then hacked them aright, and out of the beams and posts constructed a beautiful hut.

The ape had observed all this only a little while, when he said to himself, " Ho ! ho ! if it is nothing more than this, I will soon do it," and ran back to the beasts.

There arrived, he called them all together and said, " Come, come, now you shall see in me the greatest builder in the world." So he took the very best cudgel, and struck aimlessly right and left, against all the trees in all directions, so that the beasts ran out of the way. But the trees remained all quietly standing and did not stir, and the beasts laughed at him.

This made the ape angry, and he made grim faces at them. But he thought to himself, " Let

them laugh, I know more than they do, and when I
am once master, they shall feel it."

The second week, he wanted to learn how to cul-
tivate the ground, for the animals began to lack
fodder.   Then he saw, from his apple-tree, how Adam
took a spade, placed it firmly on the ground, pressed
it properly with the hand, and sunk it down in the
earth.   He also saw him afterwards tie a bag round
his body, out of which he threw various seeds into
the opened earth, in order that, in time, the grain
might grow from it.

The ape thought, "Pah! there is no art in that
—we will soon do it;" and the cunning fellow stole
secretly from Adam the spade and the seed-bag, and
ran with them back to his beasts.   "Come, come,"
he cried to them, "now you shall see what a farmer
I am."   Then he took the spade, placed it firmly
upon the earth, and pressed his hand against it with

all his might.   But instead of holding it with the iron
down, he held it turned about, the lower end up,
and, as he pressed against it, he cut his hand in two
with the sharp edge ; so he screamed aloud, and
threw away the spade.

Fortunately a dog was near, who licked the
wound, and the pain was soon gone.   Then said the
ape, " Ah, well ! the soil is but a secondary matter ;
the seed is the chief thing."   So he took the seed-
bag, and as it was empty, he filled it with little stones
and sand, bound it round his body, and walked with
an important look, and great haste, here and there,
and up and down, scattering the sand every where,
even, in his haste, into the faces of the animals.

However, after they had wiped out their eyes, .
they saw well that the wise master farmer had scattered nothing but sand in their eyes, from which no
fodder could grow in a whole lifetime.   They shook

their heads thoughtfully, and turned their backs to him.

The third week, the ape undertook to learn cooking; for it began to grow cold, and he thought if he could only prepare a warm supper for the beasts, they could never do without him again.

Then he saw how Adam put together dry brushwood, brought a brand from his house, and kindled the brushwood with it; whereupon Eve placed an earthen kettle over the fire, put the herbs in it, and at the end of an hour, the supper was ready.

"Ho, ho!" said the ape, "there is no magic in that," and, jumping from the tree, he snatched a burning chip from the fire, and, before Adam could start to follow him, he had darted with it over all the hills.

"Good appetite!" cried he to the beasts from the distance. "To-day you shall have something to eat, which all your paws will be reaching after. Hallo, you dogs; get me quickly some dry brush-wood together; then you will find out something."

The hounds brought the brushwood in haste, the ape stuck in the brand, and the flames flickered and crackled merrily in the wind. Soon, however, the flame abated. "We will soon attend to that," cried the ape, and, lying down, he blew with full cheeks in the ashes, so that the sparks flew upon his skin, and upon the beasts too, and burnt their hair. "No harm done," cried he, "no pleasure without pain, only have patience. '*End* good, *all* good.'"

Then he brought a great lettuce-leaf, strung it on two sticks over the fire, poured into it, from the hollow of his hand, water from the nearest brook, and threw into it mullen, and various herbs; whatever was at hand.

"That will relish," he cried to the hounds, from

whose jaws appetite made the water run. But scarcely had he said it, when the lettuce-leaf shrank before their eyes, the future supper ran into the fire, and put it out, and all was over with the cookery.

Then the beasts began to grumble, especially the oxen, and no one wished to know any thing more of the wisdom of the ape.

But the ape said, "Shame on you, you beasts —who lose courage so easily? If *we* do not learn, our children can. But they must be properly trained and educated for it. Therefore I will, before all things, now learn of man how to educate children."

The oxen did not agree to that, and they grumbled more than ever; but the horses and dogs, who had more love for learning, thought the plan not so bad. They persuaded the other beasts, and at the beginning of the fourth week the ape sat again upon his tree.

The little children of Eve were crying and weeping at a great rate. Their mother came out, wound them in a cloth, laid them in a round basket, and as she pushed this with her foot, so that it rocked to and fro, the children became still, and slept. The larger children, however, she kissed when they were good, and punished with blows when they were disobedient.

Scarcely had the ape seen this, when he said, "Now I understand the education of children from the foundation; but a cloth is necessary, such as men have." As such an one was hanging to dry near the apple-tree, he secretly stole it away, tied it like a banner on a stick, and went back with it in triumph to his beasts.

"Now bring all your children together at once; they shall be educated in an hour," he cried to the beasts; so they brought in haste all the young calves, colts, lambs, kids, dogs and cats, and many other young animals, some much nicer than others. The calves cried, the colts neighed, the lambs bleated, the dogs barked, the cats mewed, but, above all, the young pigs cried and squealed the loudest.

"Your screaming throats shall soon be quiet," said the ape, and he took six pigs, who cried loudest, and put them at once in the cloth, drew it together like a bundle of clothes to be washed, and laid the whole pack among the leaves of a waving bough. Thereupon he sprang himself upon the bough, and pushed with his foot upon it, in order to swing it hither and thither ; but clap-pop lay the six little pigs with their cloth upon the ground,—and all were still as mice.

"Do you see," said the ape, " I am coming gradually to understand it ?   But now I will perform my master-piece upon your elder children, and then your respect for me will increase."

Then he made all the young animals around him stand in a circle. First he looked at them a long time, with a wise and important mien ; then he went up, and kissed some of them, and licked them with his dirty lips in the tenderest manner. At last he said, "Attend ! Now comes the main point." With these words, he reached out with his broad, ell-long arms, as far as he could, and dealt boxes on the ear on all sides, so that the little creatures cried and howled loudly, and the young colts kicked and ran away.

Meanwhile the old sow had unfolded the cloth, in which her little pigs lay so still, and found that they had all six been killed by their fall, as dead as mice. The beasts thought *that* was too bad. They saw now that the ape was a vain and stupid creature, who wanted to know every thing better than any body else, but had neither patience nor desire to learn any thing in a right way. Then they drove away the foolish beast, returned to man, who had at first been appointed to be their master, and became his familiar animals.

The ape, however, still fancies that he can, *some time*, obtain dominion over the beasts, so he continually imitates whatever he sees men do.   But, since he only half begins every thing, and acts for his own sport, he is and will always be only—an ape.

When Horace had finished he said, " Mother, did you ever tell Mary that story of the little boy, which we always liked so much ? "

" I think not."

" Please tell it, Aunty," begged Mary; and Mrs. Duncan told the story of

THE LITTLE BOY WHO DID MORE THAN HE THOUGHT HE COULD.

A little boy sat early one morning at the window, with his head resting upon his hand, at last he said to

himself, " I wish I were a man, for then I might
do something to serve God, or to help others. I might
save somebody's life, or I might help the poor, or I
might cure the sick, or I might teach others to be
good. I do not see what a little child can do. But
I will try to be a good child, and to please my Father
in heaven; and he knows that I wish to serve him."

So, as he had still a little time before breakfast,
he began to study his lesson, in which he took great
delight. He was very busy at this, when he heard
his mother call to him, " Come quickly, my son, and
run after your little brother, lest he should get hurt."

" Oh dear," thought he, " I wish I could finish
this page. But no; I must obey quickly. Yes,
mamma," he said, in a pleasant voice, " I am coming;" and he hastened after his little brother. He
went out, and looked here and there after the dear
little fellow, and ran fast on the way where he thought

9

him most likely to have wandered, calling his name often, in a loud, clear voice. At last, when he was far from the house, and had begun to feel very anxious, he saw his brother running toward him as fast as his tired little feet could tottle.

Now, our little boy did not know that the dear baby was just on the edge of a rocky precipice, and at another step would have fallen over, when his voice made him stop and turn about, and that so he had saved the life of his little brother. He only knew that he tried to be an obedient child.

After breakfast, his mother told him that he might work in his flower garden. This was one of his greatest pleasures. His beds were kept in very nice order, and his plants grew fast and finely. From day to day, it was his delight to see new buds opening into full and beautiful bloom. He had one very rare plant, the seeds of which were given him by a poor woman, from a far country across the sea. This morning, for the first time, one of its buds had opened, and he called his mother to share his delight in seeing his beautiful flower. After she had left him, and he was still admiring its delicate color and sweet fragrance, a little boy passing by lingered to look at the pretty flower garden. When his eye rested on the flower just opened, he exclaimed, "Oh, that is one of the flowers of our own country! How my dear sick mother would love to see it!" And still he lingered, and looked at it longingly.

At first our little boy thought, " I should love to send it to her." Then he thought, " But I cannot part with it. I have been waiting for weeks to have that bud open." Then he looked again at the stranger boy, and saw that his face was pale and his eyes full of tears.

He asked him about his mother and his own country, and told him that the woman who gave him the seeds, came from that same land. Then he looked at his flower, and thought, "I shall soon have another bud open. I will give him this for his sick mother." So he gave away his beautiful flower.

The little boy did not know that the sick woman was the daughter of the woman who gave him the flower seeds, of whom she had heard nothing for many years, and that by that flower they were restored to each other again. He only knew that he tried to be a kind little boy.

Some hours later, he was sent by his mother on an errand to a neighbor's house. As he walked along he saw something shining in the road. He picked it up, and saw with delight that it was a beautiful silver box. Nobody was near, he could claim it as his own, and he felt as if his fortune was made. As he walked on, turning it over to admire the rich chasing, and tossing it up to feel its weight, he thought that, beautiful as it was, he would sell it, and with the money it brought he would buy a nice warm shawl for his mother, and a cloak for the dear baby. He would say nothing about it, but some day he would ask permission to go to town, and he would return at night, and surprise his mother with the new possessions. He could not help jumping up and down at the thought.

Just at that moment he saw a man on horseback coming toward him. He hastily hid his box, as if afraid of being robbed of his treasure. As they came nearer together, he saw that the man was looking intensely around on the ground, as if in search of something.

"Little boy," said he, as he came near, "have you seen a box in the road? I have lost one, not far from here."

Our little boy felt sadly to think that he must give up the box, and the shawl and the cloak, and all the joy he had been thinking about. But he did not hesitate.

"Is this the box, sir?" he asked, drawing it from his pocket.

"Yes, yes, that is it. Give it me."

So the boy gave up the box, and the man turned back, and rode away hastily, while the boy walked slowly after him. It was a sad trial to him, not for his own sake, so much as for his mother's and the baby's.

"But I did right," he said to himself, and felt cheered by the thought. "I told the truth and was honest."

He never knew that the box contained a rare and costly medicine, which restored hundreds of sick people to health.

On his return home he was caught in a heavy shower of rain, which wet him to the skin. That was not the worst of it, however, for when he reached the gate, he found that the strong wind had bent down his plants and broken off his choicest blossoms.

"Oh mother," he said as he entered the house, "my beautiful flowers are killed." And he sat down and wept.

"Who has done it, my son?" asked his mother, tenderly stroking his head.

The boy sat silent a few moments, and then he raised his head and said, "God has done it, and it is all right."

Then for the first time he saw that in the room was a stranger, who had entered for refuge from the storm.

The little boy never knew that the stranger was the Governor of the country, and that as he went away he said to himself, " God has taken *my* flowers, also, my beautiful children, and I too will say, like this child, ' It is all right;' " and that from that hour he became a better man, loving the will of God and ruling in his fear, so that the whole nation was better and happier.

He only knew that he wished to be patient and submissive.

That night when he went to bed, our little boy said to himself, " I do not know that I have *done* any good to-day, but I have tried to *be* good."

Two angels watched over his bed.   He almost saw their smiles, but he did not hear their words.

" Dear child," said the one, " who has done more than he?   Shall we not tell him? "

" Not yet," said the other; " let him wait."

After Mrs. Duncan had concluded, Horace turned to his brother: " Mr. William Duncan is called upon to contribute something to the entertainment of the evening, on the occasion of the celebration of Miss Mary Melville's birth-day. Prose or poetry, Latin or Greek, original or selected."

"That is more than I bargained for," replied William, "but I will do my best to honor the occasion."

"Read the 'Fifth Kitten,' Willy," said his mother.

"Oh yes, the 'Fifth Kitten,'" responded Horace. "Did you ever hear the 'Fifth Kitten,' Mary?"

"No, what is it?"

"You shall hear," said William, taking from the bookcase an almost worn-out newspaper, from which he read—

THE FIFTH KITTEN.

"Once there was a little girl, and her name was Emma, and it was me. And she had a great large brown cat, and her name was Hepzibah, but the little girl called her Heppy. And one day she went to give Heppy her supper, and no Heppy was there; and so I went to Heppy's bed, that she had in a box in the back kitchen, and there I saw five little wee kittens tumbling about with their eyes shut, and Heppy mewed, and the little girl took out all the kittens, and set them on the floor, and Heppy was very proud, and the little blind things bobbed about for a while, and then I put them back, and went to the parlor, and told mother. And the little girl's mother said I might keep one, and all the others must be drowned. And the little girl cried, and after supper she went to her room and sat in the dark, and thought, and thought, for nearly half an hour. And then I jumped up, and took down my slate from the nail, and wrote, " Give one kitten to Mrs. Andrews." And then I sat down, and thought and thought, and all at once another thing came into my mind, and I took the slate and wrote down, "Give another to Miss Sophronia;" that was the little girl's teacher. And then I thought again, till the clock in the little entry struck nine, and, just as it struck the ninth time, it came to me that father used to say he wanted a cat at the barn, and so I wrote that down. Then it was bed-time, and still there was one kitten left. Oh, that was a dreadful evening! I went to bed, and cried, and thought, and cried, till I found myself going to sleep, and still nothing would come into my mind about that poor little fifth kitten. And I thought, What a cruel thing you are, Emma, to go to sleep, and forget about the poor little thing that has to be drowned to-morrow. So I pinched myself till I was wide awake, and then, all of a sudden, I thought of old Hanny, by the creek, (her name is Anne, but they call her Mammy Hanny for short,) and she had four cats already, that she took from people to save them from being drowned; but I thought that she might take another, and so I felt easy in my mind, and went to sleep. And next morning, long before breakfast, I ran down to Mam Hanny, and she was not up, and the door was bolted, and she told me if I got a stick, and put it through a hole in the door, the bolt would push back, and I went in, and told Mam Hanny about the fifth kitten. And she said she had three too many now, but she would walk over and look at them, and, if there was a very pretty one, she might take it, and I told her they were all beautiful; and so she went over with me, and I took her to the back kitchen, and I put the five kittens on the floor, and Mam Hanny looked at them a great while, and at last she picked out the prettiest, and said if it had only been black, with a

white nose, and a white collar round its neck, and a
white tip on its tail, she thought she would have
kept it; and then she put on her bonnet, and all
was as bad as ever for the poor little fifth kitten.
And mother said it must be drowned, and she sent
for Jake, and he brought a big bucket from the
stable, and mother told us all to go away, and take
the poor old mother puss with us, till it was all over;
and I said no—if the darling little fifth kitten must
be killed, I knew Heppy would rather I should do
it than Jake, for Heppy couldn't bear Jake, and he
did not like Heppy. So I sent Jake away, and
mother carried Heppy to the parlor, and Hanny and
I took them all out of the box, and I did not know
what to do, for we couldn't tell which *was* the fifth
kitten; and I said, When I wrote down one for
father, I am sure I meant the brown one; and when
I wrote down one for Mrs. Andrews, I think it was

the yellow and black ; but the other three are all mixed up in my mind, and I don't see how we can tell which I meant for the fifth. And Mam Hanny said we should put the two in the box, and put the other three in my lap, and the first that crawled out should be the poor little fifth. And so we did, and I sat quite still for a good many minutes, and then the darling little white with brown ears put out its little soft paws, and travelled over my knee, and down to my foot, and rolled itself on the floor, and I sighed, and Mam Hanny sighed, and I took the darling little fifth and dropped it into the water, and I turned my back to the bucket, and Mam Hanny stood off by the wall, and shut her lips tight, and said nothing ; and all at once her face got very red, and she dashed up to the bucket, and took out the little fifth, and wiped it dry with her apron, and turned to me quite angry, and said, " Now she had five, and I

never should dare to offer her a kitten again, for she
wouldn't take it ;" and then I remembered that she
had said just that last winter, when I gave her the
gray and black with white feet. And so she left it
a few days, and then took it home, and it was the
funniest little fat thing you ever saw, and there it is
this very day, and that's all."

Mr. Duncan came in while William was reading,
and seemed to enjoy the story quite as much as any
body. He was afterwards called upon, from all
quarters, for a story.

"Well, let me see. I will tell you the wonderful
story of the Three Wishes.

"Once upon a time there were two men, who
lived opposite each other. One was very rich, and
the other was very poor. One dark night"—

Here he was interrupted by a loud ring at the
door. Mary's heart beat violently. Could it be?—

Yes, there was no mistaking her father's clear, pleasant voice. Mary rushed to the hall, and, in a moment, was in her mother's arms.

THANKSGIVING.

" Is it not time for the cars ? " asked Madam Huntingdon. " It seems to me that they are very late to-day."

" Not yet, mother," replied her daughter, Mrs. Wood. " It wants a quarter to four."

" I can scarcely realize that Charles and his family have returned. We shall surely have great cause for Thanksgiving, if they come safely back to us."

" Yes," said her husband. " It will indeed be a great blessing to have our children and children's

10

children all together in the old place. Let me see, how long has Charles been away?"

"Three years last June," replied his wife. "Little Charlotte must have changed a good deal in that time, I hope not for the worse."

"I hope not, little *tot!* I should like to have her come back just what she was when she left us. I never saw a finer child."

"A lovely child of a lovely mother. I long to see her sweet face again. I hope that her foreign education has not injured her."

"A gentleman who met them in Paris," said Mrs. Wood, "remarked that he had seldom seen a more accomplished or refined young lady. She is not sixteen yet. No! Mary is six months older, and she was sixteen in August."

"Well, I hope that they have not educated all the nature out of her," said Mr. Huntingdon, "that is the danger in these days."

"Where are Mary and the children?" asked Mrs. Huntingdon.

"Mary will be down soon," replied Mrs. Wood, who did not like to say that her daughter was giving a little extra attention to her dress, on account of the expected arrival of her cousin. "The children are playing in the orchard."

"I think I will go to the station," said Mr. H. "It is barely possible that they may come by the four o'clock train. Joseph has the horses harnessed, I believe. But don't expect them by this train, my dear," he added to his wife as he left the room.

Mary Wood, at this time, was standing before the glass in her chamber, arranging the braids of her hair. "I wonder how Lotty will be dressed," she thought. "They say she is so lady-like and genteel, and all that. I wonder if she is handsome. I suppose she talks French, and wears a watch, and has

quantities of brooches and rings and bracelets, and
perhaps wears flounced silk dresses every day, Uncle
Charles is so rich. How shabby I shall look! I
wish mother would. let me dress a little more. At
any rate I've carried my point about the hoops,"
and she glanced with satisfaction at her wide skirts,
and gave them a twitch or two, to make them set
out as much as possible.

Her thoughts went on. "It seems as if Charlotte had every thing, and I had nothing. She has
been educated in Europe, and that is so much to
tell of, and has travelled, and seen so many distinguished people,—and I suppose has every thing she
can desire, as she is an only child. She has nothing
to do but to enjoy herself; and here am I, mother
for ever denying me things, because she says she
can't afford them. She seems to think because
she sent me to New York to school, that that is

enough for my whole life, and now she wants me to teach those troublesome children, and give up every thing to them.

"Well! I suppose I must go down;" and she gave a general look at herself in the glass, and concluded that she was, after all, a handsome, fashionable-looking girl, whom perhaps her cousin Charlotte would not be ashamed of.

So she went down stairs, through the wide hall, into the large, pleasant drawing-room, where her mother and grandmother were sitting.

"Mary, dear," said her mother, "did you bring my knitting?"

"Oh dear, I forgot it, mother. Have I got to go away up stairs again?" This was said in a very impatient tone. Mrs. Wood looked uneasy. "Well, no matter, dear; it is of no consequence." Mary sat down by the table, opened her work-box, and took out her crochet-work.

"Don't you think it is too light here, grand-mama?" she asked.

"I had not thought of it, my dear; you know your grandfather likes a bright, cheerful room."

Mary looked dissatisfied. She thought "how very plain this room will look to them, with this same old furniture and carpet. If it was darker, it would hide things a little. At last she remembered that it was no more *her* grandfather's house than it was her cousin Charlotte's grandfather's, and that was quite a comfort to her.

"There is the carriage," said her grandmother. "Look, Mary, have they come?" Mary sprang to the window; "yes, there are trunks behind, and several persons inside."

"Thank God," exclaimed Madam Huntingdon, as they all hastened to the door. Mr. Huntingdon sprang from the carriage with the alacrity of a young man, and after him his son, who seemed to care for nothing till he had received his mother's welcome.

Meanwhile his father assisted Mrs. Charles, as she was called by the neighbors, and her daughter from the carriage, and on all sides they received and gave most hearty embraces. Mrs. Charles Huntingdon was that rare character—a perfect lady; she was not handsome, but there was something about her,—a sweet serenity, gentleness and dignity, which made one feel ashamed in her presence of selfishness, and passion and uncharitableness. As a rough neighbor once said of her, "It was as good as reading a sermon to look at her face."

"Little Charlotte," as she was called by the family to distinguish her from her mother, was, as her cousin Mary saw at the first glance, a person not likely to attract a stranger's admiration. She was rather short for her age, somewhat stout, with a fresh complexion, and a general look of fine health and energy. But a stranger might soon discover what a changeable, expressive face she had ; before night, Mary thought that she had never seen one which was so sweet, and so bright, and so loving. And so thought grandpapa, and so thought grandmamma.

" Well, sister, our daughters have grown up from children to young ladies since we parted," said Mr. Charles Huntingdon to Mrs. Wood, as they sat on the sofa after tea.

" Yes, three years makes a great difference at their age."

" Mary has been at Mr. N.'s ever since we went away, I think."

" Yes, she left school last summer. She has not finished the course, but I thought it better for her to spend part of her time this winter in teaching the younger ones, while she can still go on with her studies."

"You are very wise; there is nothing like teaching others, to give us assurance and command of our own knowledge. I mean that Lotty shall teach a little by-and-by."

Mary looked up in surprise: "I hope she will like it better than I do," she said, smilingly.

"Don't you like it?" asked Charlotte. "I have been almost envying you the delight of teaching Kitty and Willy. I did not remember what sweet children they are."

"They are fine children," said her father. "We have had a grand romp in the orchard. I have seen no place which looked quite so pleasant to me as this, mother. I am glad that every thing is unchanged within doors. This room, with its old furniture, is much more to my taste than modern fashions. It looks respectable, as if its owners respected themselves and their own ideas of things."

"We are too old to be running after modern fashions," said his father. "We have a good, substantial, comfortable home, and now that you and Mary and your families are together in it, we could hardly have a happier one."

"It seems a special blessing that you should be able to reach home just before Thanksgiving," said Madam Huntingdon.

"Yes, I was doubtful whether we could accomplish it. I thought it would be very pleasant to go first to the old church again, so soon after landing."

"We will take the cup of Thanksgiving, and call upon the name of the Lord," said his mother, with a calm dignity of voice and manner.

"Your good minister is well, I hope," said Mrs. Charles.

"Very well, and we may expect one of his best sermons to-morrow," said Mr. Huntingdon. "He is one of the best preachers, and best pastors, and best friends that I know of."

Then there were various inquiries made and answered about the neighbors, and the changes which time and death had made in the village.

After awhile Madam Huntingdon excused herself, as she had some household concerns which required attention; for she was too active to resign the post of housekeeper, even to Mrs. Wood.

"Cannot I help you, grandmamma?" asked Lotty, who had followed her to the hall, "I should love to."

"We'll see, my darling, thank you; I am going to send some pies and other things to some of our poor neighbors; you know that my pies have quite a reputation in the village."

"They ought to have," said Lotty, "I never ate any so good."

Grandmamma did not look displeased, and they proceeded to the kitchen.

"You remember Jenny, our old cook?" said Mrs. Huntingdon.

"Oh yes, dear grandmamma, I have seen them all; it is like getting home again."

"And, indeed, Miss Lotty did not forget us, ma'am," said Jenny; "she had not been in the house a quarter of an hour before she came to see me. And sure she has grown like the mother, God bless her."

"Who is to carry these, grandmamma?" asked Lotty.

"Joseph will take a part of them. I am going to send Susan to Mrs. Green's. She is very sick, and I want to know what she needs."

"Suppose I should go with her," said Lotty; "I think she would remember me."

"Well, darling, if you like. I am sure it would give her great pleasure. She has often inquired about you."

"But we will arrange the things for Joseph first," said Lotty. "I did not mean to run away from helping you, grandmamma."

"I am sure of that, Lotty. These roasted chickens are for Mr. Pratt, poor man! His wife died a month ago, and he is left alone with his little children; he must have a mince-pie, too. This chicken-pie is for Aunt Nelly."

"Oh! cannot Susan and I take it? It is very near Mrs. Green's. I should like to go and see the good Aunt Nelly."

"Certainly, dear, if you please, only I am afraid you will have to carry it yourself."

"Of course," said Lotty.

"And a glass of jelly with it?"

"The more the better," was the smiling reply.

"Ah, Lotty, you are my own little girl still," said her grandmother, kissing her. "This turkey and mince-pie are for our good minister. Joseph must take them when he comes back from his first trip. Now I believe we are done, my dear."

"There's the young lady for you," exclaimed Susan, on her return. "Who would have thought of her remembering old Miss Green and Aunt Nelly in them foreign parts? I thought when she gave *us* those beautiful presents, that there were few young ladies who would have thought of us. Do you believe, she brought them such nice woollen jackets, which she said she bought on purpose for them in Germany?"

"Bless her young heart," said Jenny, "I'll keep the shawl she brought me to the day of my death."

"And her mother's just like her," said Margaret.

"Yes, *them* is what I call *ladies*," said Joseph.

While these eulogies were expressed in the kitchen, the subject of them went up to the room, which she shared with Mary.

After taking off her shawl and bonnet, she was about descending to the parlor, when she heard her Aunt calling, for the third time, at the head of the stairs, "Mary—Mary dear," and for the third time Mary replied "Yes, mamma, I'll come in a moment."

"Can *I* help you, Aunty?" said Lotty.

"Oh, but you must not stop, my dear, Mr. and Mrs. Carlton and their daughters are in the parlor."

"Are they? but still I can wait a little while, and will gladly do so, if there is any thing I can do for you."

"I only wished Mary to stay with the children a few moments. Kitty is quite restless, and a little feverish, and I wished to go and prepare some medicine for her."

" Please let me stay with her, Aunty ; I think I can amuse her, and I should love to."

Her Aunt thanked and kissed her, and with a sigh, left the room. Lotty took the restless child upon her lap, and sang to her, and soothed her. Mary soon came slowly up stairs, and in the dim light did not perceive that it was Lotty.

" What do you want, mamma ? " she asked in an impatient tone.

" It is I, Mary," said Lotty, softly. " I do not think she wants you now."

" I was talking with Mr. Carlton," said Mary, " and could not leave him sooner. They are wondering where you are, Lotty. Let me take Kitty while you go down. Come to sister, Kitty." Kitty hesitated.

" Yes, Kitty, now I must go," said Lotty. " Give cousin Lotty a kiss, and to-morrow I hope you will be well enough to go to church with me. Good night, darling."

"Good night, darling," replied the child.

Mary took her little sister in her arms, feeling very much ashamed of herself.

And this was cousin Lotty, this simple, loving, self-forgetting girl! Nobody would guess that she had been educated in Europe, or that her father was very rich, or that she had nothing in the world to do but to enjoy herself. How plainly she was dressed; how cordial and sympathising she was with the least and lowest—how little she seemed to think of herself in any way. What did people mean by speaking of her as so accomplished and refined? She certainly had not a fashionable air. She would not be distinguished in company, and yet there was a grace which seemed to come from within, pervading all she said and did, which won all hearts to her.

11

"I wish I was like her," thought Mary. "How different I am," and with the feeling she drew her little sister closer to her and kissed her. "Dear little Kitty, what can sister do for you?"

"Sing—like Lotty," whispered Kitty. Mary was a fine singer, though she had valued her superiority in that respect chiefly as a means of winning the admiration of strangers. Now with a low, sweet voice she sung to her little sister, until the child slept sweetly in her arms, and so her mother found her on her return.

"Are you here still, Lotty?" whispered Mrs. Wood.

"No, mamma, it is I," said Mary.

A few minutes earlier her mother would have found her in another mood; mortification, or impatience, or jealousy might have triumphed over better feelings, but now she spoke gently and affectionately.

"I am sorry, mamma dear, that I was so long in coming. Mr. Carlton was talking with me, but still I might have come. Now won't you go down, mother? I will stay with Kitty. I would rather."

"If you wish it, my dear," said her mother; "I should like to see Mr. and Mrs. Carlton."

"How inconsiderate and selfish I have been," Mary thought, after her mother left her, "as if mother did not want to see her old friends, and as if they did not want to see her more than such a forward, insignificant thing as I am! If I ever do such a thing again I'll——"

She was angry with herself, and in her vehemence moved so as to disturb little Kitty, who moaned and turned her head. Mary soothed her very tenderly, till the child slept again, and then laid her upon the bed, and sat beside it, giving way to humbler and gentle feelings.

After awhile she heard the piano. "Lotty is going to play and sing," she said to herself; "some Italian or German music, I suppose."

She was mistaken. Lotty was playing at her grandfather's request at family worship, and her father's and mother's voices accompanied hers in the old hymn,

"When all thy mercies, Oh! my God," &c.

Soon afterwards Lotty came up to her room, where Mary joined her, when her mother had relieved her of her charge, and had assured her that she had no need of her offered assistance during the night.

"You do not wear a hoop, Lotty," said Mary, as they undressed.

"No," said Lotty, "mamma said she would rather I would not."

"Don't you like them?" asked Mary.

"I am perfectly willing to have mamma settle such matters for me," said Lotty evasively; "it saves me a great deal of trouble," she added smiling.

Mary scarcely knew what to make of such entire indifference to fashion, or of such entire deference to a mother's opinion.

"What a beautiful watch! May I look at it, Lotty?"

"Certainly. It was a birth-day present from papa. We happened to be at Geneva on my birth-day."

It was a beautiful little hunting-watch, attached to a black cord, without ornament of any kind.

"Nobody would know she wore a watch," thought Mary, "and she wears no bracelets, and only one ring, and that simple brooch, with hair in it."

"Nobody would think!" "Anybody would think!"

"What would people think!" These words, which had such power over Mary, had very little weight with Lotty.

"What is right?" "What will God approve?" —were the motives which, at least, she *wished* to govern her in all things. And so, without considering what Mary "would think," but simply following her own habit, she knelt by the bed-side, and said her evening prayer.

Mary did not soon fall asleep. She felt rebuked, not by any thing in Lotty's words or manner to herself, which were kind and affectionate. There was nothing about her which said "I am holier than thou!" On the contrary, she was so self-forgetting, so free, so simple, so overflowing with spirits, that she seemed almost a child.

Long after Lotty had given her the good-night kiss, which she felt scarcely worthy to receive, she lay awake, wishing that she was like her.

"I will try to be like her," was Mary's last conscious feeling that night.

Little Kitty was so much improved by morning, that she could sit at the breakfast table, next to cousin Lotty.

"I should think that the prodigal son had come home, mother, and you had killed for him the fatted calf," said Mr. Charles Huntingdon, glancing over the plentiful table.

"One dearer and more welcome than a prodigal," replied his mother.

"That is rather against scripture, my dear," said her husband.

There were pleasant, though sad memories of former thanksgiving days, when others long departed had been with them. The aged pair had buried six of their eight children, most of them in childhood, and now Mr. Charles H. and Mrs. Wood were all. Mrs. Wood's husband had died six years before, two of her children had soon followed him, and she had afterwards come to live with her parents.

Mr. and Mrs. Charles, too, had been bereaved; their only son had been taken from them in the beauty and promise of early childhood, and since then their affection and care had centred upon Lotty, who well repaid it all.

Mr. Huntingdon's pew was well filled at the morning service. The venerable man, erect and dignified, with his white flowing hair, the tall and beautiful old lady, whose face told every stranger of the peace and kindness of her heart, their daughter, in her garments of widowhood, with her gentle, chastened look; her little children, in fresh health and beauty; and Mary, certainly with no ordinary attractions of face and person; Mr. Charles H. with his fine face and noble air, and his wife and daughter, so refined and elegant,—this group would have attracted the attention of a stranger. It certainly was regarded by their neighbors with no slight degree of interest and admiration.

There were sincere worshippers in that family pew. Hearty and humble thanks from parents and children went up to God for all his mercies, and especially for this happy reunion after their long separation. Mary was impressed by the reverence of her cousin's manner. There was no looking about, no glances inquiring for friends whom Lotty was of too affectionate and ardent a nature to have forgotten to think of with interest; neither was there any display of the deep emotion which she felt; she was perfectly calm and attentive to the service, as if her heart was in it.

After church, she saluted her many old friends

with a cordial and almost gay delight. Mary saw that she did nothing for effect, that every thing about her was truthful and genuine ; and she felt for her a respect almost amounting to reverence.

She knew and realized how different she herself was ; seeking for admiration, aiming to please every-body, always thinking of herself and what would be thought of her. She never before had been so conscious of these faults, and she despised them.

"I think that this is the best part of Thanksgiving," said little Willy, as he seated himself at the dinner table.

"You do, do you, little man ?" said his uncle, patting his curly head, "well, it is a pretty good part of it, no doubt."

And so they all seemed to think, and so they had good reason to think, so far as boiled turkey, and roasted ducks, and plum-pudding, and mince-pie, and all attendant luxuries could furnish reason. Every one seemed in fine spirits. Mr. and Mrs. Huntingdon were almost as merry as Willy and Kitty; and the good man glanced around his well-spread table, upon children and grandchildren, with loving pride. There might have been other families met together that day, whose joy had less of sad and chastening remembrances, but there were none where was felt a more true and loving thanksgiving, one which did not forget bereavement and sorrow, but which was led by them to a higher faith and a serener joy.

Early in the evening, while the older members of the family were talking over the past, the children had coaxed Lotty into a corner of the room to play with them. Willy wanted her to fight with him, with the set of tin soldiers she had brought him from Germany, and Kitty wanted her to play paper-dolls.

" Would you rather have the English or the Russians ?" asked Willy.

" Which would you ? "

" Oh ! I like the English best, and they will beat of course ; but you may have them if you want them."

" No ; I'll have the Russians, and see how bravely they will fight," said Lotty.

" One of the cannon is broken ; " said Willy, " it won't shoot."

" That's no matter ;" replied Lotty, " let the English shoot awhile with the good one, and then lend it to the Russians ; I think that would be a good way in real battles."

" Do you ? " said Willy.

" Yes, it would be very obliging for the enemies to lend their cannon to each other ; I don't think half so many people would be killed ! "

" You are a funny girl," said Willy. So they had a great fight, shooting by turns, with the little peas from the one cannon. The English conquered, of course, which Willy supposed was owing to their good cause, united with his successful generalship.

"Now will you play paper-dolls?" asked Kitty.

"If you will tell me how. Why, what a quantity you have of them!"

"Yes; I have got fourteen children. There are three pairs of twins; I think it's real fun to have twins, don't you?"

"I suppose it is," said Lotty; "do you dress them all alike?"'

"Yes, but it takes a great deal of cloth; I have to buy two pieces of de laine for their dresses."

"You must be very rich!"

"Oh, I am! and I have to keep so many nurses for them, and I dress the nurses all alike too. I have just been making the children some travelling dresses; are not they pretty brown dresses with blue capes, and flats trimmed with blue?"

"They are beautiful," said Lotty; "why, how pretty they are!"

"Now let us play," said Kitty; "will you choose the ones you like best? Which would you rather have of these two?"

Lotty selected a fat, red-cheeked little image.

"That is Ellen; well, now, choose some more."

A one-sided thing, named Grace, was the next choice; at last Lotty found herself in possession of seven children, including a pair of twins.

"Now what are we to do?" she asked.

"Suppose we dress them in their walking dresses, and take them out to see the soldiers."

"What?"

"To see Willy's soldiers!"

Lotty laughed and consented.

The little images were dressed in pink, with white jackets, and hats trimmed with pink, and seemed to enjoy the soldiers as much as most children of their size. Little Bessie fell down and tore her dress; Flora was accidentally shot by a cannon ball, which broke her leg; and Rosa got lost behind a hill, which looked like a work-box; but at last they all returned safely home, where their seven nurses were waiting for them, sitting in a row, all dressed in brown, with white aprons and neckerchiefs.

"Now we will put them to bed," said Lotty; "have they any night-clothes?"

"To be sure: do you suppose I should let my children go without night-gowns? You will find them in their drawers; I call the envelopes their drawers."

So the dolls were undressed, and put to bed in the envelopes, and all the envelopes put in a box. The Russians and English also ceased hostilities, and encamped for the night, after having collected their stray cannon-balls for future use.

Then the whole family, grandmamma and all, had some merry games with the children,—" blindman's buff," and " hunt the slipper," and " lading the ship," and " proverbs," until it was time for the little ones to go to bed.

Grandmamma proposed having some music, and Mr. Charles II. asked Mary to play. She hesitated at first, thinking of Lotty's superior advantages; but she recollected that Lotty would not hesitate for such a reason, and she sat down to the piano and did as well as she could.

" You are an excellent player," said Mrs. Charles, with her sweet smile, when Mary had finished her first piece.

" Very good indeed," said her husband; " now you must sing."

Mary sang well, though with a slightly affected manner.

"Her musical talents must be cultivated," said Mr. Charles H. to his sister; "we must have her in New York, and she and Mary can improve each other, under some good teacher."

The evening passed rapidly away, with music and conversation, and bed-time came very early, as it seemed to all. Mr. and Mrs. Charles Huntingdon and Lotty were to leave in the morning for their long-deserted New York home, where many things required their immediate presence.

"I suppose we must not complain of our short visit, or urge a longer one at present," said Madam H.; "we will try to come again at Christmas, and you will go back with us, I hope, all of you."

This pleasant plan was readily agreed to. The morning train took the travellers to New York, to re-establish themselves in their own happy home.

"Is not cousin Lotty nice?" asked Kitty as they

12

drove away; " she plays paper dolls as well as a little
girl ! "

" And she plays soldiers as well as a little boy,"
said Willy.

What grandpapa and grandmamma and Aunt
Wood said is not recorded.   What Mary said was
nothing ; what she thought was a great deal ; and all
her life afterwards she had happy cause to remember
her cousin Lotty and that Thanksgiving day.

THE CHRISTMAS TREE.

To my children, as to most others, Christmas was a long-expected day. For weeks beforehand, great were their plans and contrivances. Unusual tasks were performed, and sacrifices made, for the sake of increasing their store of pocket-money. Mary even seriously proposed that I should pay her sixpence a week, if she would give up ice-creams, which in the country, and in the depth of winter, was rather an imaginary self-denial. I asked the little lady if she would not like to be paid for not going to the moon.

My good Aunt Esther had come to spend the

winter with us. In her view, the observance of Christmas was very objectionable. "If it was not Popish and superstitious," she said, "it was certainly making too light of sacred things. It is well proved that Christ was *not* born on that day, and, even if we were sure that he was, it should be kept in a solemn manner, and not as a day of sport and merriment. I respected her scruples, but in answer to them rose up my own well-remembered childish feelings of gratitude and joy, and more vivid recognition upon that day of the Saviour born upon the earth. And in later years, it has been a delightful thought to me that thousands of children, in many lands, were rejoicing together in the birth of the holy child Jesus. It is well to commemorate the event, even if we have no certainty in regard to the day. The Reconciler and Redeemer has come, and we have a right to be glad.

For the first time in our family, a Christmas tree was to be substituted for the immemorial custom of "hanging up stockings." Uncle Charles had recently returned from Germany, with glowing recollections of its happy and friendly homes. With some difficulty, the children were won over to the new project. Mary thought that "Christmas would not be Christmas," if she did not hang up her stocking; but on recalling to mind that some presents in past years had been none the less valued, because too large to be contained in a stocking, she gave up the point, and thought it would be well enough for once. Grace thought that "half the fun" was in getting up before light, to discover the unknown treasures. But on considering that the tree would produce the same things over night, and they would still be in her possession in the morning, and moreover, that she might rise at midnight if she chose, and disturb

the family as usual with her good wishes, she too
gave in to the new system. Philly had been its
warm advocate from the first. He had read, and
Uncle Charles had told him, too, of the German
children, dancing in delight around the brilliant,
decorated tree, and it was a bright vision to his
young imagination. "It would be almost like seeing a fairy."

Christmas was to be on Thursday. On the previous Saturday afternoon, the children's half-holiday,
the tree was selected. At two o'clock the "double
sleigh" was at the door. Romeo and Cæsar, the
two well-beloved horses, were in fine spirits, tossing
their heads, and making the bells jingle in their impatience. It was no small matter to pack in the
children and their elders. Aunt Esther and myself
sat on the back seat, with Gracie, wrapped up like a
little old woman, between us. In fact, the children

all looked like bundles of cloaks and furs, for there was little to be seen of any thing else, except some bright eyes peeping out. Philly had on a fur cap, which turned down and covered his ears, and a great comforter round his neck. Mary sat next to him, in the middle of the front seat. Uncle Charles, and John, the man, tucked them all up in the warm buffalo skins, drawing one so close over Mary and Philly, that only their heads were left visible, and those so enveloped, that they could not turn them, but had to look straight forward. But that is one of the pleasures of a country sleighride.

Then Uncle Charles shook the snow from his boots, and wedged himself, the best way he could, into the small space left, next to "little Mother Bunch," as he called Mary. He drew the buffalo skin around him, took the reins from John, and the two fleet horses started off, as if they too enjoyed the keen bright air, the glittering snow, the rapid motion, and the jingling bells.

The sleighing was what Philly called "first-rate," the snow deep, hard-frozen, and well-trodden. There was a little danger now and then of an upset, in turning out in the woods for the farmers' sleds, well laden with hay. They kept behind one for a time, till they came to a good place to turn out, and the restrained horses took bites at the fragrant load before their noses; and the wind, too, constantly took little wisps of it in his sharp teeth, scattering them along the road, marking the farmer's path, so that it would be very easy to tell which way he had gone, if he should get lost, and his wife should send after him.

They came at last to a thick grove of firs, very near the road. What a beautiful sight it was to see those dark evergreens growing out of the pure, untrodden snow! Here they stopped, and selected the Christmas tree. It was a straight, handsome fir, about eight feet high, with broad-spread, regular boughs. Uncle Charles notched it with a hatchet he had brought, so that John, who was to cut it down and bring it on the sled, might make no mistake. This operation was watched very earnestly by six bright eyes.

Then Uncle Charles stepped into the sleigh again, and after a drive, which seemed very short, they were safe at home again, talking and laughing around the parlor fire.

Now, of what happened between that time and Christmas, I am not going to tell you, for so many secrets were confided to me, that I could hardly tell any thing without betraying somebody. So we will come at once to Christmas eve.

The family were all in the front parlor, which

was a very comfortable and pleasant room. The curtains were down, and a bright wood fire crackling and glowing in the fire-place, which looked very cheerful, with its white hearth and polished brasses. The folding-doors were closed, but the children looked toward them very often. There were papa, and mamma, and Aunt Esther, who was mamma's aunt, and Uncle Charles, who was mamma's brother, and Uncle Henry and Aunt Susan, papa's brother and his wife, with their four children, Fred, and Anna, and Caro, and little Henry. Then there were Mr. and Mrs. Lee, our minister and his wife. Altogether we made a good room full.

Uncle Charles and myself went out of the room for a while, and the children, too expectant to entertain themselves, asked their papa to tell them a story. "Well, sit down then. I can't tell a story to a flock of pigeons." Whereupon the flock of pigeons screamed, spread their many-colored wings, and after a little fluttering, at last alighted in something like a straight row on the carpet. When they became quiet enough, their father told them the following true story :—

"There was once a little German boy, whose father was dead, and his mother very poor. The German children say that the *Christkind* (or little child Jesus) comes down from heaven, and brings their Christmas gifts. This little boy believed it, and so he thought he would ask the Christkind to bring him what he wanted most, which was a good warm cloak for his mother, and some wooden soldiers and a trumpet for himself. To make sure that the Christkind should know his wishes, he wrote him a letter, telling him of them. He directed the letter 'to the Christkind up in heaven;' and carried it to the post-office. When Christmas eve had come, the little boy sat down before the fire, holding in his hand a little sprig of fir, for he was too poor to have a tree.   He prayed silently to the Christkind to grant his request.   While he was praying, the door opened, and a man in a long cloak entered, laid a bundle on the table, and went away without saying a word. When the boy opened the bundle, he found, to be sure, the very things he had wanted."   "*Did* the Christkind bring them?" asked Gracie.   "The Christkind *sent* them," said her father, "and I will tell you how.   Some clerks at the post-office seeing the strange direction on the letter, opened it, and instead of laughing at the ignorant boy, they kindly agreed among themselves that they would provide the things for him.   Perhaps they loved the Saviour, and were happy to do it in his stead, or rather, to have him do it through them."   Gracie's eyes filled with tears, and Philly said, "How happy they must have been!"

At that moment the folding doors opened, and a brilliant, beautiful sight presented itself. In the middle of the room, in a large box, stood the Christmas tree, its dark green boughs illuminated with a profusion of wax tapers. It was ornamented with fancy papers of different colors, curiously cut, and hung in tasteful festoons. Apples, covered with gilding in various devices, oranges, grapes, frosted cakes, and tempting confectionary hung from its branches. No tree but a Christmas tree ever bore so many kinds of fruit. Slippers, watch-cases, needle-books, and real books, a whole set of furniture, and a whole train of cars were also among its productions. There was a crying baby, and a screaming parrot, and a barking dog, which Uncle Charles would now and then slily set to performing their various vocations. I was greatly pleased with a pin-cushion with my own name upon it, for it showed me that little Mary had tried to improve in her needle-work. I noticed that among Fred's presents was a very pretty ball from Philly. A few weeks before, Philly had by accident thrown Fred's ball, an old one, into a well, and although it was drawn out, it looked much worse than before. I observed, too, that the very prettiest presents of all the children were given to cousin Caro, a sweet little girl of four, who had broken her arm a few weeks previous, and was still weak and delicate. Mr. Lee received from the united forces of the children of both families, (to say nothing of Aunt Sally's busy fingers,) a nice warm dressing-gown, much to his apparent satisfaction. Indeed, he looked as if he could hardly help putting it on, at once. Mrs. Lee looked equally pleased, at receiving from the same source a pretty work-box, well furnished. But I cannot tell you all, though I must not forget to say, that their papa's present from the children was, an excellent daguerreotype of the three little rogues, taken under Uncle Charles's auspices, and with considerable aid from his purse. It had been a tremendous effort to keep this secret. Just as they were starting on the important business their papa met them, and asked where they were going. The children were in great perturbation, but Uncle Charles smilingly answered, "Oh, it is a great secret," and they passed out. Fortunately, their father forgot to question them afterwards.

Aunt Esther had occasion to think well of this Christmas at least, and looked very kindly upon it, through her new gold-bowed spectacles, such as she had never possessed before.

Another thing I must not forget to mention, Dinah, our cook, was a colored woman, who had lived with us many years, and was greatly esteemed and beloved by us all, for her many Christian virtues. The children had purchased for her a handsome Testament, with clear paper and large print, and had her name printed in gilt letters on the cover. On the fly-leaf their names were written, with the date, "Christmas, 1854." Accompanying each name was a verse selected by the children. Mary chose the verse " God so loved the world that he sent his only-begotten Son, that whosoever believeth on Him, should not perish, but have everlasting life." Philly's was, "Thanks be unto God for his unspeakable gift;" and little Grace's was, " Wherefore if God so loved us, we ought also to love one another." The dear old woman received it with tears of joy, and blessings on their precious heads.

But Christmas eve must come to an end. Dinah and Jenny and John were called, none of whom had been neglected in the distribution. Jenny, indeed, was already wearing her pretty new collar, the children's gift; and John, somehow or other, had frequent occasion to use one of his new silk pocket-handkerchiefs. Mr. Lee borrowed Dinah's Testament, and the whole circle listened reverently, while he read the beautiful chapter of the nativity, telling of the shepherds watching their flocks by night, and of the multitude of the heavenly host singing " Glory to God, peace on earth, and good-will toward men," and of the birth of the heavenly babe.   Then we all sang the hymn "While shepherds watched their flocks by night."   It was very pleasant to sing it all together, parents and children, old and young, while the rich voice of good old Dinah told of a heart full of humble and sweet devotion.   Then we all knelt down, and in simple but earnest words, our good pastor offered thanksgiving for all the blessings of that day, but mostly for the great gift of God's love to each one of us, and to the whole human race, in all ages, and fervently prayed that each one there present might live for the kingdom of the great

13

Prince of Peace, and that to our hearts, and to all hearts, might come the blessings of which the angels sang.

Soon after, the sleigh-bells were jingling at the door, and there was a great bustle in finding and appropriating the numberless articles of out-door comfort. In a little time our guests were all gone, and the three happy, but tired-out children fast asleep. Aunt Esther and Uncle Charles put out the wax tapers and soon followed, the former candidly remarking as she took her candle, that "there *was something* in keeping Christmas, after all." Papa and mamma saw that all was safe, and went together to look, tearful and prayerful, at the fair faces of their sleeping children.

THE OLD YEAR.

The Old year paused when his race was run,
And his last day's pilgrimage was done.
Twelve long months he had held his way
Onward, onward, by night and day ;
Caring not for the cares of earth,
Mirthful not with its scenes of mirth ;
" Hasting not, resting not," on he went,
Like a star in the lofty firmament.

He started forth at the dead of night,
An old man, robed in the purest white,

With a long gray beard, and a hoary head,
With a clear bright eye, and a stately tread,
His noble stature by age unbent,
And thus for months on his way he went.
Then, as he journeyed, he cast away
His robe of white, and his beard so gray;
With buds and blossoms he wreathed his head,
And a bright green mantle around him spread.
To greet his coming the flowrets sprang,
And the air with the birds' glad music rang;
For the foot which trampled to dust again,
The budding hopes of the sons of men,
The foot which hurried with careless stride
O'er the ruins of human love and pride—
That foot passed on with its soft quick tread,
Calling each blossom from sylvan bed,
Waking to life, as at second birth,
The bright and beautiful forms of earth.

Then with a graceful, yet firmer tread,
With lilies and vine-leaves garlanded,

The wanderer passed in his silent race,
O'er many a lovely and verdant place,
Giving earth's treasures a brighter bloom,
Giving man's treasures full often a tomb,
Bathing all nature in richer light,
Shrouding full often the heart in night;
Silently keeping his destined way,
Onward he journeyed by night and day.

Then he left behind his wreath of flowers,
With the balmy air and the shady bowers,
And wove a garland, his brow to suit,
Of purple leaves and of golden fruit.
The foliage sere in his pathway fell,
Telling of sorrow and death too well.
But he heeded not what hope or joy
His reckless footsteps might destroy;
His path was marked, and he trod the way,
Whether through sunlight or shade it lay.
When he had well-nigh run his race,
And saw before him his resting-place,

He donned the garment of white once more,
And the long gray beard which he had before.
At last he paused, for his race was run,
And his last day's pilgrimage was done.
Cold, and silence, and night had sway,
When that strange old wanderer passed away:
Stern and silent as night and snow,
None could follow, or see him go;
Yet men were silent, and bowed the head,
As if the soul of a king had fled.

Though the silent wanderer took no part
In the joys and cares of the human heart,
Yet where is the untouched spirit, where,
To which he brought not or joy, or care?
Never an eye on his form was cast,
As in silence and awfulness on he past,
That saw again what it saw before,
When it turned its glances to earth once more.
There is not on earth a single spot,
Which the print of his footstep beareth not.

In the heart's most secret and silent place
Has that fearful stranger left his trace;
On all that he passed, on all that he met,
The print of his mystic seal was set,
And the impress of that signet strange,
Its wondrous motto, was one word—"*change.*"
Ah! who can read, with an eye undim,
The stamp which that wanderer left on him?
He passed o'er all ere his work was done,
All save the throne of the Changeless One!

Ah! but the few who drew boldly near,
And walked at the side of the stern Old Year,
In his mantled form, in his moveless face,
Saw heavenly beauty, divinest grace;—
That his calm clear glance, undimmed by tears,
Took in all ages, and countless spheres;
That his tireless step, so firm and strong,
Moved to the movements of heavenly song;
Knew that sublime was the path he trod,
Girt by angels, and straight to God.

And so they followed where'er he led,
'Mid ruins, deserts, and graves of the dead;
With lofty hope, and without a fear,
They kept by the side of that good Old Year.